OTHER BOOKS BY GEORGETTE KAPLAN

The Woman at the Edge of Town
Ex-Wives of Dracula

The Scissor Link Series
Scissor Link
Face It

The Cushing-Nevada Chronicles
Easy Nevada and the Pyramid's Curse
Candice Cushing and the Lost Tomb of Cleopatra
You, Me, and the Sunken Treasure

You, Me, and the Sunken Treasure

Georgette Kaplan

PROLOGUE

A HORRIBLE THOUGHT CAME TO Easy Nevada as she dreamt, and the horrible thought was that she wasn't dreaming.

She dreamed of the pyramid, the betrayal—Candice's face as they took her away—and she dreamed of the desert sifting past with mocking monotony. Its features rearranged themselves around her; every dune she walked over circled around and placed itself back in front of her. Every mote of sand she coughed up came back into her lungs with ten friends.

She dreamed of the comparative health and haleness she'd had after Singh and his right-hand attack dog John Gore had left her for dead just south of the middle of the fucking Sahara. All het up on revenge, she could've run a marathon then. She'd buried Candice's grandfather—who'd been killed protecting Nevada so that she could protect his family—and taken the horse of a dead Khamsin along with a gun and three bullets.

She'd put all three into the horse after it couldn't go any farther. Why should it suffer? She'd been the one who'd made all the mistakes.

She was still dreaming of walking. Shouldn't she have woken up by now?

Time melted in the desert. The only way Nevada could tell it was passing was her tongue swelling in her mouth—a slug trying to crawl down her throat. Her lips blackening and cracking. Her throat closing. Everything wet in her body drying into hard leather. She forgot the feeling of having saliva in her mouth. She forgot the stability of having anything under her feet but shifting sands. She forgot her own name. But she kept walking until she couldn't anymore. Then she crawled.

When she couldn't even do that, she fell and finally felt cool.

CHAPTER 1

"Sir, Mr. Gore is on the line for you."

Singh wrenched himself away from the window where he'd been resting his head. He pulled the sleep mask off and took in his surroundings: the limousine, its gentle vibrations as its tires dominated the road; the dire view out of the tinted windows; and the open partition to the front seat, where the passenger-side bodyguard had a phone pressed to his chest.

"Did you tell him I'm napping?" Singh demanded, wiping the crud from his eyes. "It's very important I get my sleep, you know. I was hoping we'd be out of this godforsaken country by the time I woke up. Now I'm going to have to—I don't even know. The internet here is shit. I want to play Candy Crush, but I can't find it on my phone and I can't download it again and—"

"Sir, Gore said to give you twenty seconds and then put him through."

Singh sighed. "Fine. Hold the phone up to my face, I still have something in my eye." He wiped at the corner of it as his bodyguard held the phone out to him. "Not that close! I haven't moisturized in a while. I want a respectful distance. Back, back, back!"

His bodyguard pulled the phone back. After a few feet, Singh gave a stiff nod and the bodyguard activated the video chat. Gore filled the screen, looking so fresh and professional it was irritating.

"Yes, Gore, what do you want?"

"I took the liberty of dispatching a team into the desert, after Nevada."

"You said she couldn't survive. That she wouldn't last a day."

"I like to be sure. It makes me happy."

Singh scratched his chin. "So, how is she?"

"That's just it. We don't know. They couldn't find her."

"Maybe some wild animals got her."

"It's the Sahara," Gore said dubiously.

Singh blew air between his lips. "Well, she couldn't have gotten far. Find her."

"We're trying, sir. But as I said, it's the Sahara."

Singh chewed the inside of his cheek. Stress, stress, stress. First no Candy Crush, now this. "Maybe she's learned her lesson and now she's taking a load off in Aruba."

Gore acted like he didn't even hear. "I'll keep looking."

"So… She's not dead. You don't know where she is. And, *ergo*, you don't know what she's planning? Then all you've managed to accomplish by telling me this is to stress me out."

Gore blinked. "I thought you might want to know."

"Well, I don't! If she's in the next room with a knife and she wants to kill me, then I'd like to know! But what if she's just behind a sand dune, dead, and you couldn't find her because you're not looking hard enough? Then I'll have stressed myself out for nothing. No, I refuse to worry about this. You, *you*, worry about it. That's what I'm paying you for. I'm going back to sleep. *You* stay awake."

"It's 2 PM," Gore said.

"Then I've only had a forty-five-minute nap. Don't expect me to apologize for being grouchy when I've only had forty-five minutes of sleep." Singh pulled his sleep mask back on. "Find Nevada. She's in a desert. What could she possibly be doing to hide from you?"

"This seems rather gratuitous," Candice said as she worked the stripper pole.

It was hardly necessary—she wore a pleated skirt that came down to just below her crotch and a white dress shirt that was both unbuttoned to show off her cleavage and tied up to show off her midriff. Standing still would've been enough for almost anyone's sexual appetites, but she ground against the pole, circled it to show her body off from every angle, shimmied up and down it so that none of her exposed skin could possibly be missed.

Nevada sat at the foot of the stage drinking a Bloody Mary. "I'm American. I don't know the meaning of the word. Literally. Is it a kind of fruit?"

Candice gripped the necktie she was wearing and twined it around the pole. "You're a lesbian. I thought you liked function."

"I can think of several functions for you," Nevada argued.

The club's atmosphere was oppressively erotic—dimly lit to begin with, neon signs blaring to show off exposed skin in exotic shades. If Nevada wanted to see Candice's natural coloring, she'd have to get her somewhere private, but for the moment, she was content to enjoy her company here. The speakers growled out Haddaway's "What Is Love" loud enough to be another partner on the dance floor.

Nevada swilled her drink, the taste intense enough to linger in her mouth like someone had kissed her. "I know it's kitschy, but I legit like this song. What *is* love?"

Candice's tongue flashed out of her mouth and ran up the stripper pole, the saliva trail glowing with each pulse of the neon lights. Nevada thought about how unlike Candice it was to do something so unsanitary.

Like she'd read her mind, Candice said, "You do know you're dreaming, yeah?"

"Of course I know I'm asleep!" Nevada retorted instantly, crossing her arms even if it made a little of her Bloody Mary slosh out. "Maybe if you showed a little skin…"

Candice hung off the pole, looking upside down at Nevada before jolting upright and driving herself against it with a domineering thrust. She pushed her ass out with the same conquering energy, like she knew Nevada's eyes were being pulled to her tartan skirt as it drew up the curve of her buttocks. Nevada saw the lowermost whiteness where cotton panties covered Candice's groin.

"Have you given any thought to what you're going to do when you wake up?" Candice asked. The panties flashed down her inner thighs, painted red as blood by a neon throb, and then they slid down her long legs.

Nevada leaned forward to see more. She knew that the panties really made no difference when Candice's skirt was in the way, but in her heart, it looked different. The skirt clung tighter to Candice's curving buttocks, delved deeper into the valley between her cheeks. She could see a hint of the flesh that joined Candice's legs together—shadows providing a tempting target for the glowing neon—and her lips felt *dry, bone-dry, and cracked like the ground after an earthquake, a taste of blood the only moisture…*

Nevada took another sip of her Bloody Mary. "What will I do when I wake up? Find you, kill Singh... make my dreams come true."

Candice straightened her skirt with a dainty tug of her fingers. "Yeah, that's not going to happen. I know I'm a black woman, but do you really think I have an ass like this?"

She gave her ass a slap that had the bass turned all the way up.

"Maybe if you bent over more, I could say for sure."

Still with her back to Nevada—every curve of it—Candice reached to her chest and undid the few buttons that passed for modesty. Her blouse opened, pulled to either side by her spreading hands, and Candice twisted at the hip. Her open blouse wasn't totally transparent, but Nevada saw the shadow of the side of her breast, the heft, the jiggle—all but the fine golden coloring that made her look truly delectable.

"Is there a worse phrase in the English language than *side boob*?" Nevada waxed philosophically.

Candice hung onto the pole as she slid down to the floor, landing in a tangle of crossing limbs and artfully concealed nudity like she'd *fallen down the side of a dune, sand burning her skin like a rain of boiling water, the night cold doing nothing to cool her when fever was frying her like an egg.*

Nevada tried to take a drink. Empty. "Service!" she called, shaking the celery inside the glass. "Where were we?"

"Racial stereotypes," Candice said, coming to all fours, prowling to Nevada over a floor of shifting colors, everything changing but her eyes.

"Right. I think we're breaking those. You know, most people would say a black woman couldn't be a Japanese schoolgirl."

"I thought I was Catholic."

"Correcting me in my subconscious? That's a new one."

Candice padded onto Nevada's table, neon flashing over her so fast that Nevada only caught glimpses. Her skin was creamy, taut with muscle tone, but no chiseled abs, no bulging biceps—no scars. Everything about her was as soft and smooth as a *drink of water being forced down her throat, Nevada gagging on it, her body rebelling against being awakened when it was so close to mercifully shutting down.*

Candice swiped Nevada's drink away from her. It was full again, the Mary so bloody that it ran down the sides. "Find your boss. Kill your boss. Get the girl."

"It is the American Dream," Nevada said. She reached for the glass, but Candice pulled it away before she could close her hand around it. Her fingers came away red with dripping condensation.

"You always did like a challenge," Candice said.

"That sounds like a note of criticism in your voice. But it could just be your voice."

"It's not a criticism. It's an observation." Candice drank. Her lips dripped red. "You don't want to see the world as denials and dead ends, so you look at it as challenges. Quests. Finding the artifact. Going on the adventure." She smiled. Her teeth were red too. "Seducing the girl."

"You think that's all you are to me? A challenge?"

"You tell me. It's your subconscious."

"You're a subconscious," Nevada retorted in a snit.

"That's what I just said."

"Very negative. Lots of negativity."

"Not really." Candice grew serious. "If I were really being negative, I'd ask you what you expect to happen when you rescue me—assuming you find me, get past the private army, climb the mountain and all that. Do you really think I'll want anything to do with you after you got me into all this?"

"You wanted to come!" Nevada protested. "It was your idea!"

"Keep telling yourself that," Candice said. "Since you are literally telling yourself that."

"God, all these years of people telling me I should be self-aware, I try it once and it blows. Why am I dreaming about you, anyway? I have an entire US Women's Soccer Team to choose from."

Candice grinned—raking Nevada's mind over memories of how sunny her smile was, how it curved, how it showed her teeth, how it came so easily when she was pleased. "You're dreaming of me because you miss me."

"Yeah," Nevada said dismally. There was no point in arguing. She'd never been much good at talking herself out of anything.

"The real question," Candice said, "is: am *I* dreaming of *you*?"

Awakening pummeled Nevada, aches and pains slamming into her consciousness like a car crash. She moaned and tried to get comfortable.

All she cared about was pulling herself into a position that didn't exacerbate her pain. She rolled onto her side, held herself, and tried to breathe evenly enough not to aggravate anything.

It took long minutes, but the pain faded to a dull roar under her skin. She took stock of her body. Wiggled her toes, flexed her fingers. Nothing felt broken. Cracked maybe, definitely bruised, but she was in one half-dead piece.

For a moment, everything that'd happened seemed like a horrible dream. She felt Candice's presence so vividly that when she forced her eyes open, she expected to see Candice lying next to her. But there was nothing but haze in front of her eyes. She spared a moment to think of Usama, hoping he was at peace.

I don't really know much about Islam, but I hope you're having a good time in heaven with Allah and his… son?… Mohammed?

Fuck it.

She planted her fists below her and hauled herself up, gritting her teeth against the fresh wave of pain that hit her. It almost made her nauseous, her skull feeling both heady and airy at the same time, but she managed. The world was softer than she remembered—she was sitting on a mattress. Rescued.

She looked around.

Black bodies surrounded her. They looked like she felt. Dressed either in shabby donations, old fashions, and worn fabric, or cheap Wal-Mart chic. They looked cowed, tails between their legs, and as Nevada's vision swam into focus, it was easy to see why. Bruises, lacerations—they were a pack of beaten dogs, half-starved as well.

None of them paid much attention to her. Prison rules—*keep your head down and it won't get smacked down.* Most weren't speaking, but when they were, it was in low, hushed conversation. Nevada couldn't really listen—the blood pounded in her ears too thickly—but she recognized snatches of Bambara, Hausa, Buduma, Akan. Nothing she was particularly fluent in, but a smorgasbord of languages from Equatorial Africa. What were they all doing here?

She looked over their surroundings. A large common room, dozens of cots lining the walls, benches and a table running down the center of the room. Mudbrick walls, sandy floors. She was still in the fucking desert.

It looked familiar, though. That gave her a headache, her mind another muscle strained and overused, but as she looked around, she placed the familiarity. Jacques had told her enough stories about the French Foreign Legion to recognize the shelves over the beds, the hanging cupboards, the air of distilled misery. This was a fort. Old, abandoned, put to a use its builders had never intended, but still an outpost of the Tricolor. And she was in the barracks.

She noticed a presence at the side of her cot, a puffball of curly black hair pushing up from behind the mattress. Nevada craned her neck until she saw the small child, no taller than her cot, staring at her.

"Yo, Don King, what're you looking at?"

He replied in a patois far too fast and grammatically loose for her to detect more than some English DNA in it. Her headache felt worse.

"Okay, I didn't catch any of that, but you're like six, so I'm guessing you're talking about Fortnite?"

"He's asking you why your skin is white." A man's voice, with an accent Nevada wanted to place as… Mali?

"Tell him I grew up next to some power lines."

The man was tall, slender, his limbs sprawling out from sloping shoulders and narrow hips. He had an affinity for the thrift store clothing, making him look more like a hipster than a hobo. Coming to Nevada's bedside, he presented his hands. Wide palms, delicate fingers.

"I used to be a doctor," he explained.

Nevada held out her arm and let him take her pulse. "Where are we?"

"Somewhere in Algeria, by my reckoning."

"Algeria," Nevada repeated a little woozily. The effort of conversation tired her quickly. She had to force herself to stay awake.

The kid said something, watching as the doctor examined Nevada's eyes.

"He says you smell funny," the doctor said, not looking up from her healing wounds. Nevada noticed as he went over them that the bandages were clean enough to have been changed recently.

"We don't have to translate everything he says," she replied. "Tell him it's Chanel No. 5. It's an institution." She saw an IV line running from her arm to a saline drip on the shelf over her bed, where some long-dead legionnaire had kept his cleaning bag. "Jesus…"

"You are coming along nicely," the doctor said. He sat on Nevada's cot, shy of her hip. "When we found you, you were in and out, life and death. Dehydration, exposure. Very bad. We took you with us, and for the last two days, here you have slept. Oh. I am rude. My name is Sy Savant."

"Pleasure to meet you," Nevada said. "More or less… Hey, Doc? This might be a cultural difference, but I assume when people are sleeping three to a cot, something's not gone according to plan?"

Savant nodded. "We were meant to leave for Europe yesterday. They are keeping us here. Some tried to leave, but…"

"How many are there? Keeping you here?"

Savant looked to have misgivings about answering. Before he could decide either way, a booming *crack* shot through the barracks. A whole chorus of them assaulted the ear, and every man in the room shot to his feet, standing tall, almost *en pointe*, hands behind their backs, eyes looking straight ahead.

Prison rules. Can I call them, or can I call them?

They came in wearing desert camouflage and blue headscarves. Arabs armed with thick, black clubs and leather shields, pounding both together. Tuaregs, Nevada guessed from the geometric patterns on their shields. They could've been family heirlooms centuries old. The clubs, though, were stun batons.

As Nevada watched, Savant caught a guard's notice. The guard advanced on him, berating him. Nevada couldn't understand the language, but she got the meaning. The guard thought he was being eyeballed. Savant quaked, trying to hold himself still, like if he could make a statue of himself, he would be spared a beating.

The guard jabbed his baton into Savant's chest; blue sparks shot out as it fed an electric current into his trembling body. The hyena cackle of the stun charge was loud, but it couldn't compete with the physical vibration of Savant's body seizing up, teeth set together, muscles locked, his flesh now a prison he was locked in.

The guard pulled his baton back and Savant collapsed, a puppet without strings. Then the beating started. Kicks. Stomps. The guard venting aggression, savoring the release—he might as well have been going at a punching bag.

"Hey!" Nevada called. "Why don't you pick on somebody your own gender?"

The guard stopped to look at her. The others stared too.

"I'm calling you a woman," Nevada explained. "It's an insult. I'm being insulting… Lay off, okay? I just woke up."

The guards surrounded her, sensing a threat in her mockery. Some stared at her balefully for the challenge, while others felt too much lust to be offended. Nevada girded herself for a fight, throwing aside the sheets to free up her body. Then she realized what she was wearing.

"Why the fuck am I dressed like Princess Jasmine on her honeymoon?"

She was in full bedlah—a bejeweled bra, a vest, and either harem pants or some kind of gauzy skirt. She couldn't really tell the difference.

One of the guards triggered his stun baton. Electricity flickered between the prongs on the business end. "Come quietly."

"You sound like my college roommate." Nevada rolled out of bed. The guards surrounded her, stun batons at the ready, shields held high. "What do you think I'm gonna do, belly dance you to death? C'mon. Take me to your leader."

She tried to hold her vest closed as they walked her out of the barracks. The heat smashed down on her, the sun stung her eyes—same old, same old. This was definitely a Legion fort, but not one any picky archaeologist would be interested in. The French had not left the place to move to the suburbs. The gates were blown off their hinges, with fragments of the heavy wood lying in the doorway, so badly burnt they looked like they could've still been smoldering. That passage was impossible to go through, but a hole blasted in the wall let people move in and out. Through it, Nevada saw a Quonset hut, its interior filled with crates, trucks, jeeps. *A smuggling operation.* It made sense. Get the migrants to buy a ticket, then tell them their seat's taken by whatever you're really shipping.

Sand grew over the place like a cancer, piling high and spilling out of windows. The architects hadn't wracked their brains coming up with designs. It was four tall walls, walkways running over them for defenders to repel attackers. Mudbrick cabins ran along the walls: canteen, armory, kitchen. An array of stairs led into the cabins and over them, up to the wall walks. But battle damage had blown out the stairs in several places, as well as the cabin roofs that served as landings—they were replaced with planks and ladders to make the spaces somewhat passable. It all seemed vaguely postapocalyptic, but then, Nevada had always thought one person's apocalypse was another person's Tuesday.

Between the walls, the courtyard was fifty square feet of dead sand. There was a stage and a twenty-by-twenty iron cage, empty, the open lock ringing against the door as it was blown by the wind. In the northwest corner, a tower rose past the thirty-foot walls, shooting above the battlements to provide a lookout platform. Beside it, a water tower balanced on four legs.

The guards led Nevada between the naked struts and into the tower beneath the lookout platform: an empty space of stairs turning their way up to an exit out onto the wall walks and further circling around to a door. Nevada got a shove in the back and trudged up the stone stairs. In places, the treads were gone completely, replaced by planks spanning the gaps, which bowed threateningly when she put her weight on them.

"You guys talk to OSHA about getting an inspector out here?" she asked the guards. "Everyone deserves a safe workplace."

They didn't answer. Like David Hasselhoff, no one appreciated her outside of Germany.

They forced her up, up, up, a strenuous task when her body was still working its way up to solid food. Nevada didn't mind. It worked the kinks out, snapped her bones back into position. She felt energy trickling back into her, like she was thawing out after a long winter.

Finally they arrived at the door. A guard reached past Nevada to knock on it. A moment later, the door opened, and Nevada was face to face with a fez.

The man was short, broad, and bloated in the middle, wearing dark sunglasses and a suit the color of mayonnaise gone bad. His skin was lightly perfumed with sweat, carrying its florid scent directly to Nevada's nose, and as soon as he'd opened the door, he beat a retreat back to his desk, where a fan hummed away.

"Come in!" he chattered in a slightly marble-mouthed Cairo accent. "In, in, in! I've been anxiously awaiting your awaking. Yes, very good. I can see you are feeling well."

A stun baton jammed into her back, not charged, but she felt the cool metal prongs through her thin vest. Nevada went in, noting that two guards followed her inside, closing the door and standing by it.

"Don't worry about them," the man continued. "Their English is, ah, nonexistent. Isn't it, you fatheads? You bumpkins!" He smiled at Nevada, displaying teeth as small and fine as pearls inside an oyster. "We can speak freely. And eat!"

He gestured with sudden casualness to an old-fashioned loo table, set up with a newfangled folding chair for maximum discrepancy. On it, though, was a feast. Nevada's stomach had been a tight ball of hunger for so long that she'd fenced it in at the back of her mind, but the sight, the smell of actual food brought it roaring back. She hunched over the table and stuffed herself, not able to decipher any of the ingredients or the meals they'd been mixed into, not caring. The typical Arab spices burnt her tongue, but she didn't care about that either, except to look at the man and mumble, "Water!" with her mouth full.

He chuckled knowingly and walked to a window, opening the shutters to reveal the water tower right next door. Several planks had been ripped out of the tank so he could reach right over with a pitcher and fill it up. He brought it over to Nevada—allowing her to see the days of beard growth giving him a stubble like something that grew on cheese if you left it out too long—and poured it into a cup. Nevada drank greedily.

"You are a vision of loveliness," he said as Nevada chugged from the cup and water ran down her chin. "A woman of great passions, of hunger! I have been keeping an eye open for a woman such as you."

Now that her mouth was no longer on fire, Nevada started in on the flatbread things and the bean things. "You want to start a podcast?"

"I think you misunderstand. First, allow me to introduce myself. I am Ahmed Fedil, at your service."

Nevada met his eyes while drinking in the room. The garrison commander had lived here once, if she didn't miss her guess, but scavengers and souvenir hunters had stripped the place to the bone. Outlines marked where frames had hung and furniture had sat—now as pale as Hiroshima shadows. Fedil didn't seem to mind the skeletal quality of his surroundings. This place was a way station, not a destination.

"Easy Nevada," she supplied.

"Easy," he repeated, rolling the word on his tongue. Apparently it didn't taste like a noun. "Unusual name."

"My parents lived in Hollywood. Why am I dressed like a gritty reboot of *I Dream of Jeannie*?"

Fedil picked up a stool from below the window and moved it to the opposite side of the loo table. Nevada watched him sit down across from her, feeling a canine growl welling in her. If he reached for any of her food...

"Let me explain that with a story," Fedil began, folding his hands across his belly.

Nevada shut her eyes. Great. She'd been taken hostage by Aristotle.

"You've heard of the garbageman, yes? He goes from house to house, collecting refuse."

"Rings a bell," Nevada said. She forced her eyes open enough to see what she was eating. She was hungry enough to start in on the table if she didn't know any better.

Pleased, Fedil rattled his fingers on top of the table. "Very good. The garbageman, he takes the refuse, he disposes of it. It's worthless, it's useless. Imagine, then, that one day he finds a diamond among the waste. Of course, though it would be his job to be rid of it with the rest of the trash, he would much rather keep it. This treasure."

Nevada felt his smile on her like a layer of grease. "I'm the treasure."

"Very much so. And you could have a fine life with me, a pleasurable life. There would be servants for the cooking and cleaning, of course. You wouldn't sully your hands with such tripe. No, you are meant for more passionate pursuits. Tell me—are you aware of a rusty trombone?"

Nevada took a deep breath. "Listen, Ahmed—can I call you Ahmed? You're a really great guy and you've taught me so much about inner beauty and you're going to make some girl just so happy... but I think we should just be friends."

Fedil's eyebrows contorted like dying caterpillars. "You are spurning me."

"'Fraid so. It's not you, it's me. See, in my country, slavery is kinda considered... passé? I mean, unless you have an internship..."

Fedil shot up to his full height; it didn't take long. "Then you will be sold with the rest of this scum! I am sure a white woman will fetch a high price!"

"We are pretty great."

"Guards!" They leapt to attention. "Get her out of my sight! Take her to the auction block and be rid of her immediately!"

Nevada glugged down her water before the guards could seize her. As they dragged her away, she shouted, "Joke's on all y'all. I'm Liam Neeson's daughter. You're so screwed!"

CHAPTER 2

They led Nevada down the stairs and out into the courtyard, past the sawtooth shadows of the crenellated walls above and into the thick, stuffy air of the Sahara day.

"We fight," Nevada said, sweat instantly breaking out on her forehead, "but deep down we really care about each other."

It took work to make water a bad thing in the lashing heat of the desert, but they accomplished it. As Nevada was led to the cage in the center of the courtyard, now stuffed with the captives from the barracks, the guards started up a pump. Its rhythmic chugging irritated Nevada's ears, instantly putting her on edge. She looked over at the pipe that ran down from the water tower, the machine pulling its contents down and pushing them out a hose. The water flowed out of the hose in a rushing stream, hitting the cage like an artillery blast.

The water was unstoppable, driving into them, heedless of their screams, knocking them back, shoving them down, forcing them to claw over each other for protection. It ripped their clothes, burnished their bodies into obsidian, and exploded into foam that they scrambled to drink as much as avoid. Watching the frenzy—the satisfied sneers that the guards wore as they reassured themselves of their own cruelty—Nevada wondered what Candice was going through. Her hand tightened into a fist. She felt her knuckles shifting like tectonic plates in an earthquake, vibrating, needing the solidness of slamming into bone...

The hose cut off, drips of water lost into steam upon touching the burning sand. The cacophony of rushing water and frightened screams became quiet, almost background noise. Whimpering and sobs.

"If you're going to power-wash me," Nevada said to the guards, "you have to use spring water. I have allergies and break out if you use tap. You know there won't be a mortician in the world good enough to let you have an open-casket funeral, right?"

More shoving. They unlocked the chain, hauled the door open, and threw her in. Nevada turned and, pro forma, gripped the bars as the lock clunked back into place. She rattled them. There was something easy in the way they took her shaking.

Some of the others picked themselves up, wrung out their clothes—but many simply stayed where they had fallen. Nevada nodded to them. "How's it going, fellow slaves?"

She returned her attention to the prison bars. They were loose in their moorings. Not enough to make a damned bit of difference, but still enough to be telling.

The slavers couldn't keep their merchandise out in the sun all day. They'd lose too many to heatstroke, dehydration—it'd cut into their profit margins. That would explain the barracks. They could stow the slaves there indefinitely and bring them out here for the auctions. Stuff them into the cage, wash them up—that meant the buyers would be here soon.

It also meant this cage had seen a lot of turnover. Saturated with cold water, dried in the sun, exposed to piss, sweat, the weight of the leaning slaves—Nevada wasn't a scientist, but she doubted any of that was an improvement on Brasso. Touching the bars, she could feel they weren't smooth but *rough*, scratchy even, rust abrading every bar in at least one place. She couldn't count on Fedil being incompetent enough to let his prison rust away to nothingness—Nevada knew her luck better than that—but maybe there'd been enough degradation for her to make a point.

"Is it just me or was TripAdvisor way too easy on this place?" Nevada circled the cage, running her hand over the bars and seeing how firmly they stayed in place. "Now, I'm not the kind of woman who asks to speak to a manager, but the service here? I feel like the breakfast buffet was very oversold, the TVs don't even get premium channels, and I don't know about you, but my wine was served room temperature." She scowled. "Let's call it on this place and go to a Holiday Inn."

Savant spoke first—not that it was a close race. "You want to escape?"

"That's what I was getting at, yeah." Nevada paused. The bar she was passing had shifted when she'd pressed it. She scratched it with her thumbnail, and the outermost layer of iron came off in dandruff flakes. "Maybe I was being too clever. I like to phrase things good and stuff."

"If we try to escape, they will shoot us."

"If you don't try, you'll be a slave. It's a bad career choice. Lousy hours. No dental."

"It is the only option," Savant said firmly. "Escape is impossible."

Nevada fixed him with her strongest stare, pushing into his mind with all the willpower at her disposal. "*Nothing* is impossible."

She threw her elbow backward. It crashed through the loose bar, popping it out of the cell and down to the sand. Nevada stooped down to pick it up and offered it to Savant. "Hide this. Tell the others to be ready. When I give the signal, go apeshit. And, uh… stand in front of me while you translate?"

Savant still seemed bowled over by holding the prison bar in his hand. The question wrinkled his brow further. "Why?"

Nevada stepped behind him. She rubbed her elbow. "That was very cool and sexy of me, but it *really hurt*!"

Pulling her tendons to the snapping point, she managed to wrench out another three bars while the guards weren't looking. *They* were busy erecting a large canopy and setting up rows of folding chairs underneath.

There was no place for Nevada to store even one prison bar, but they'd make good clubs for the other prisoners. If she could get them in a position to use them.

"The Foreign Legion, she is *misère game*," Jacques had told her once. "They take the miserable, heap miseries upon them, situate them in *distilleries de la souffrance*, and then distribute that misery to those miserable enough to have the scorn of *le coq* upon them. *Viva la France*!"

Nevada hadn't understood half of that, but the fort was definitely living up to its reputation as a distillery of misery. Maybe it was just her. Usually at times like this, she could focus entirely on her goal, almost willing what she wanted closer and closer until she could finally reach it. She couldn't do that now. She kept thinking of Candice and where she was and what was happening to her. Singh had her, and Nevada could only think of what he would do to get what he wanted. It gave her a rancid feeling—there wasn't any getting clean until she got Candice back.

Sound carried far in the desert. Nevada heard the trucks coming from a long way off. She looked at the thirty imprisoned with her, seeing if there were any cues for her to pick up on, but this was new for all of them. She stretched and popped the kinks out of her neck. No way of knowing what was coming, but when it did, she had a feeling it would happen fast.

The trucks stopped outside the crack in the wall. Nevada saw the sand kicked up, heard the hiss of engines cooling. Doors opening, boots pounding the sand. Abruptly, a guard filled her vision. He raised his AK-47 over his head and fired into the air, the shell casings tumbling down around his feet. Nevada dutifully covered her ears. The others cowered. Nevada didn't blame them. It was a hard sound to get used to. No more bullets. Sudden silence. It lingered almost long enough to become comfortable before Nevada heard the shunt of the key in the cage's lock, the rasp of metal being forced together. Four-man team. One opened the door, one covered the action with the AK, the other two went in with stun batons and dragged the first unlucky bastard out. A good, clean operation. They'd only made one mistake.

The door shut again. Locked. The slave didn't resist as he was forced across the courtyard, up onto the podium. It was only ten feet away. Nevada had a good look at him being forced up the steps and propped there like a centerpiece—positioned by the guards so they wouldn't be holding him in place, but he'd damn sure be where they wanted him to be.

Fedil's voice rang out with salesmanship as he led his clients in through the cracked wall. "Big, strong boys for your fields, pretty women for your houses, a few children—ah, this one here, a digger. Big, big, big, he'll work all day. What am I bid? Five hundred? Five hundred dinars, I cannot take less…"

Anonymous men followed him, dressed like they were on safari. Cotton khakis, even pith helmets. They drank heavily from ubiquitous plastic water bottles as they were wanded by the guards and parted from their guns and anything that made a loud noise going into an empty barrel. And right in the middle of them, big as life, was Jacques. He could dry-clean his suit, he could buy a new hat, he could even shave, but Nevada would know Jacques's mismatched face anywhere. She could've danced a jig.

"Six fifty!" Fedil crowed from the dais, his happiness souring Nevada's. "Do I hear seven hundred? We are going once, we are going twice! Sold to Mister Six, thank you, and wise of all of you to save your money. The best is yet to come."

Stooping, Nevada reached between the bars and grabbed the empty shell casings. She held them in her palm, working her hand in and out of a fist as the guards came again. Aimed into the cage, opened the door, moved like sharks for their chosen target, until Nevada stepped in the way. She felt the assault rifle bearing down on her, stun batons poised with their venomous charge almost touching her skin. She didn't move.

"Why save the best for last?" she asked cordially.

The guard racked the bolt on his rifle. Nevada's life flashed before her eyes. She remembered that Otis Graham owed her twenty bucks and had never paid her back. Then Fedil called out, with ingratiating slickness, something to paper over the incident. The guards took hold of her and directed her up to the dais with as much pageantry as a prisoner walking to the electric chair.

"We are off to a slow start," Fedil continued in English, "and it may prove to be a long day. So let us get things moving with a special surprise for you gentlemen. As you can see, this woman is not meant for factories, for farming, for the housework—she is meant to be a queen. Gentlemen, I give you Desert Flower, a pearl that could only be formed under the light of a full moon!"

Where was this guy when I was writing my OkCupid profile? Nevada wondered. She stopped on the dais, three guards arranged behind and to either side of her. Eyes landed on her like a cloud of mosquitos.

"Of course, much as I would love to give each of you loyal customers a gift as sweet as this, only one of you can receive her," Fedil boasted. "So let you show which will be most appreciative. Let us start bidding at ten thousand dinar!"

Nevada hummed consideringly. The other guy had sold for about five hundred American dollars. She'd made it into the quadruple digits right off the bat. Being sold into slavery was proving surprisingly good for her self-esteem.

Weeds sprung up in untended gardens with the same mindless tenacity that the customers bid for her. The words had no rancor in them, no obscenity—just the coolly restrained excitement of the bidding. Nonetheless, they pawed at her, followed the course set by their lustful eyes in eating the flesh from her bones. There was a resentment there: for her youth, her beauty, her pride, and each shouted number was meant to chisel away at the target of the hatred. Nevada didn't know if she could've taken it so calmly without knowing Jacques was there to be her escape plan. As it was, it made for an interesting experience, but not one she'd recommend. Way too much like working retail for her taste.

Jacques's voice rose above the fray: "What are you trying to pull here?"

The sudden harshness of his shout brought the auction to a standstill. Before anyone could think of what to say, he had pushed his way through the crowd, coming up to where Nevada was on display.

"Look at her," he insisted, gesturing at Nevada as though he were trying to draw a waiter's attention to some glaring difficulty with his order—it being on fire, for instance. "This is meant to be a bedwarmer for a discerning customer such as oneself? I don't know about the others, but I may have a woman for free as I like. If I am to pay, I expect top quality. And yet, what's this? She is cross-eyed!"

Nevada obligingly crossed her eyes, telling herself that once she was done avenging herself on Singh and Gore, she would deal with Jacques. *You can't just pay full price, can you? You have to haggle...*

"Not that I mean to be exacting," Jacques demurred. "*Dites donc*, one cannot expect perfection. But look how she drools. Is it too much to ask that in a desert, one may keep dry?"

Nevada let some spit loll out before whispering to Jacques, "Take it down a notch, will you? You're not going to get them to give you a free toaster too."

Jacques nodded. "And she has bad breath! *Épouvantable!* I will pay seven thousand dinar, as the Good Lord asks us to be charitable, but not one penny more!"

Silence spread out from his last word, the force of Jacques's personality daring anyone to disagree with his assessment of Nevada. He eyeballed the crowd, and the slavers looked among themselves, but no one was willing to counteract him. Nevada couldn't help but feel a little offended.

"You might mention I have a great personality," she muttered.

"Why be dishonest?" Jacques whispered back.

Fedil, eager to move things along from this lull, clapped his hands together. "Very well—the customer is always right. Seven thousand from Mister Four. But surely, a few minor flaws cannot detract from the fiery soul of this woman! Who will give me eight thousand? Do I hear eight thousand?"

This must be what being on The Bachelor *feels like. That's my bucket list done.*

Fedil didn't like the taste of seven thousand dinars, but he stomached it. "Seven thousand goes once, seven thousand goes twice—"

"Twenty thousand dinars."

The man spoke in a cool, clear voice that made up for in willpower what it lacked in volume. Eyes followed the sound like iron fillings to a magnet. The tall man with the noble bearing, the brutal face, the eyes that were sharp as razors and full of revenge. Nevada recognized him. Hadn't she had killed his son?

"Twenty thousand dinars," repeated Nazir al-Jabbar. "For the slow death of Easy Nevada."

CHAPTER 3

It was almost gratifying, the terror these self-styled masters of the world suddenly showed in Nazir's presence. Nevada could see they were filthy with fear, glancing around to see if anyone was going to make a run for it, or maybe attack and give them the chance to get away. This had to be how stampedes started, when a lion wandered up to the watering hole.

"That is a very generous offer. A generous offer indeed," Fedil said, signaling his men to search Nazir. He lobbed endless pleasantries that hit with all the stopping power of confetti, but his patter smoothed over the wait as his man wanded Nazir. The metal detector revealed a sidearm. Nazir took out a Heckler & Koch P9S from its holster and took out the magazine, handing it over to Fedil's security. He kept the pistol.

"There's still one in the pipe, you idiot," Nevada muttered under her breath, squeezing on the spent bullets like 7.62mm stress balls. With the mob's attention on the interplay between Fedil and Nazir, she quickly traded whispers with Jacques. "You have enough to outbid him?"

"I *might*," Jacques said, his voice flooding with bitterness, "if the drugs I had been smuggling were not *stolen*!"

"Can the *j'accuse* act; it was like a year ago."

"It was last week!"

Nevada risked meeting his eyes, conveying with a glance that this could be hashed out later. He calmed and looked away again.

"We'll have to go to Plan B," she said.

"How darling it would be for Plan A to work for once. Just once." Jacques's eyes traced over Nevada and her outfit. "I always preferred *Bewitched* myself."

Fedil and Nazir had sorted out introductions. They walked up to the dais, practically arm in arm, while two of Nazir's black-clad men took up position at the entrance to the fort. They held a brace of heavy chains. If Nazir won the auction, Nevada got the feeling she wouldn't be going with them under the honor system.

"Thea Quatermain," Nazir said as he came up to her, spreading his hands in greeting. "As far as I'm concerned, you're already bought and paid for. I'm merely here for the handoff."

"Nazir, always nice to see you," she replied. "How're the kids?"

"This time I feel you are much closer to God's plan for you. Not a hero. Only another American cowboy who thinks she can solve the world's problems with a lasso and a six-shooter."

"My gun's got a lot more than six shots," Nevada retorted.

"You think your petty quips hide the tininess of you… the futility… but I see through it. The scared little girl who thinks she can make herself big by pretending to be… what? Arnold Schwarzenegger? Sylvester Stallone?"

"Actually, I was always kinda partial to Bruce Willis." Nevada felt her adrenaline rising like gorge—an urge to do something, anything, so long as there was movement, a chance for salvation, or at least to bloody her knuckles before she went down. It took willpower to simply stand there and smile at Nazir, but when there was a shark in the water, it was better to smile than splash around like a wounded seal. "Can I be honest? You're over. You're done. You're like the Wilhelm scream. We get it. The whole Muslim terrorist thing is very last fall. We've moved on. We have Russians and North Koreans now, and sometimes Mexicans. You need to rebrand, give yourself a makeover. Maybe do a gender swap, add a black guy, some musical numbers, I don't know. But right now, you're about as relevant as MySpace."

Nazir's eyes blazed as they focused on Fedil. "Conclude the bidding. You can see the need to teach her proper respect."

"Twenty thousand dinars," Fedil said a bit numbly. "Do I hear twenty-one?"

Nevada shot Jacques an emphatic look. He hopped to. "Twenty-one thousand."

Nazir scrutinized him. "I don't believe this man has twenty-one thousand dinars. He looks like he doesn't even have a laundry machine."

"Hey," Nevada insisted, "you know the last thing to go through your son's head?"

"Thirty thousand dinar," Nazir growled at Fedil, anger roughening his voice like something was scratching its way out of him. "Do not accept any more bids from the Frenchman. *Give her to me now*!"

"Last thing to go through Farouq's head," Nevada continued. "Probably the caboose."

The next few moments proceeded with the spine-tingling slowness of a roller coaster cresting a hill. Nazir's right hand dove into his robes, going for the bulge of his holstered gun. Nevada had seconds to act, but she was already in motion, reacting almost before Nazir's first twitch. As he brought the P9S out of his shoulder holster, Nevada's left hand chopped into his wrist, deadening every nerve in his hand. The P9S slipped out of his grip and hung in the air.

Nevada's adrenaline surged, and the roller coaster went downhill. She caught the P9S in her right hand and brought it up, the bottomless pit of the muzzle now sucking at the fear on Nazir's face. Her adrenaline shook inside her like a living thing—she nearly killed him just for the hell of it.

"Nazir al-Jabbar, prepare to meet Allah… in hell!"

She pivoted, gripping the P9S in both hands, moving so fast that even the oven-hot air of the Sahara felt cool on her skin. She came to a stop, the silent roar of the gun barrel trained on the cage as she gave it voice. The one round chambered in the gun flew out, the bark of its launch giving way to the aria of it cutting through the air, ending in a crescendo as it hit the lock on the door.

The lock fell in two pieces, hitting the sand with a muffled thud, as ordinary as a cough after an opera.

The slaves charged out of the open door. The Tuareg guards fought back an explosion. *Bzzt*—the electrical charge from a baton drove a slave nearly out of his skin. Another slave went after the same guard; the Tuareg's shield knocked him back with a ringing *clang*. A third slave tackled the guard to the ground, and then a fourth and a fifth came to stomp their tormentor into the sand. And the same thing happened for twenty feet in every direction. One slave waded into the bidders swinging a prison bar, and blood flew from every arcing blow.

Nevada ignored it—background noise. She focused on Nazir. Rammed herself into him and drove the slide-locked pistol into his skull. It sounded beautiful, like an axe splitting lumber. He went sprawling, his motion only checked by running into a guard. A guard with a pistol in his holster and blood pouring down his face. Nazir ripped the pistol from his holster and swung around to face Nevada. She didn't have time to think of last words before her vision flashed silver. A sword swiped past her face with Jacques on the other end of it. Then Nazir stood before her, his face a rictus of pain and shock, gaze fixed on his gun hand, detached from his wrist and laying by his feet.

"I guess you were just here for the hand off," Nevada said. She charged to finish him off but was slammed sideways by the struggling bodies of a guard and a slave. The ground rose up to hit her and snatch the gun away from her. She raised her head to see Nazir clutching his wounded arm to his chest and speeding in the other direction. Jacques yanked her to her feet before boots could land on her face.

"It is possible we have overstayed our welcome," he said, driving his sword into the nearest guard and surrendering it to the pull of the body cavity.

Nevada saw ten of Nazir's men coming through the gap in the wall, shoving and clubbing aside everyone in their path as they drove through the battleground. She turned the other way to find a Tuareg shoving a gun in her face.

"Don't you need these to make that work?" she asked, opening her hand and flashing him the spent shells.

He instinctively checked his weapon. Nevada swiped it out of his hands and used it to put his jaw at a permanently different angle.

"Jacques, quit playing with the sword. Here!" He stopped trying to pull the sword out of the dead guard long enough for Nevada to toss him the gun. "Go bring the car around."

Jacques checked the clip automatically. "What about you?" he asked, still sounding uncommitted to that plan.

Nevada shined a grin on him. "With an outfit like this, you let the dress do all the work."

Jacques shrugged. "You know, that Allah thing was not even a little theologically accurate."

"Hey, I get enough of that from Candice." She gave Jacques a shove. "*Go*!"

She took her own advice, running *away* from the exit, keeping the riot between herself and Nazir's men. Her only chance was to scale the walls, maybe work her way back around to the gap, and get outside the fort and to whatever transportation Jacques had handy. But as she ran, the shock of the breakout gave way to the Tuaregs' training. Sentries posted on the walls fired down into the crowd; Fedil yelled at them not to damage his rebellious merchandise or to hit him. More guards burst out of the fort's cool interior right in front of Nevada, making her the first thing they saw as they came out into the blistering heat.

Nevada thought fast. She jabbed her hand at the battle, shouting one of the commands she'd heard repeated frequently by the guards. Hopefully it was something along the lines of *Go! Now!*

Keyed up and given to ask questions never, the Tuaregs obeyed her directions, running past her in a rush of garishly painted shields and humming stun batons. It was only the last guard in line who wondered why he was taking orders from a woman dressed like she danced for Jabba the Hutt.

Nevada cringed. "What gave me away?"

He lunged. His stun baton shot out at Nevada. She caught the blow, her hands on the shaft of his baton and his forearm. The sizzling prongs of the taser stopped an inch from her face. She could see the blue sparks of its electricity through her eyelids when she blinked. He strained to drive the baton forward enough to make contact, but Nevada locked her muscles against him. He brought the shield in his other hand up to club her side. She ignored it as best she could, even as each clobbering blow wracked her sore ribs.

Footsteps behind her, a straggler running to join the reinforcements. Nevada barely heard him over the blood thundering in her ears, but she caught his footsteps stopping in the doorway as he gaped at the scene before him. Then they moved double-time, pounding the sand behind her. Nevada's muscles burned more with each second, the pain of the battering shield taxing her concentration—she felt like a terrier fighting a junkyard dog, her only advantage a tenacious determination to hang on. Finally, the other guard was upon them.

Nevada flowed to one side, shifting her weight to the right as she redirected the baton to the left. Without her resistance, the stun baton drove past her face and into the second guard, delivering its charge right into his chest. As he shook with the voltage, Nevada whipped her freed hands down to *his* baton and jammed it into the first guard. They trembled as they electrocuted each other.

"Try to contain your shock." Nevada grabbed both stun batons. Freed of the electrical charge that had held them paralyzed, the two guards collapsed against each other like a pair of drunks staggering home.

Carrying both batons, Nevada rushed into the mess room. The dank coolness was so different from the desert outside that it flash-froze the sweat on her skin. Stairs led to a second floor and took her through a trapdoor. She ended up in a barracks where the night shift roused to the debacle outside. Four men. All with stun batons.

There was no running the same scam twice. In her getup, she obviously wasn't supposed to be there. Two of the half-dressed Tuaregs came at her at once. Nevada parried them, hammering their batons down with her own. The other two guards were only a hair slower. They brought their batons down on Nevada's, trapping her weapons between theirs.

Nevada circled to the left, trying to free her batons. They circled to the right, keeping them trapped. She reversed course and went right; they went left. She backed up and they charged her, holding her batons in place as the wall loomed behind her.

The instant before she hit, Nevada jumped, kicking back with her feet. She rebounded off the wall and into the four men, tackling them to the ground in a sprawl of bodies. Nevada recovered first. She jammed her two batons into the nearest two men and taught them a new dance move. The other two attacked, and Nevada collared them both with the batons and drew their heads together. With two slashing swings from her batons, they went down with broken jaws.

The trapdoor hinges creaked behind her. Nevada whirled to see one of Nazir's men coming through. She threw a baton end over end, and he slammed the trapdoor shut again to shield himself. Nevada threw herself toward the nearest bunk bed, overturning it on top of the trapdoor. She ran the other way. Two of the Tuaregs were getting up. Nevada swung her remaining baton like a baseball bat as she passed. One's head rebounded into the other's with a noise like a blacksmith at work.

She ran up two flights of stairs, emerging onto the roof. The harsh sunlight gouged at her eyes. The sunbaked roof scorched her through her sandals. In front of her, there was a four-story drop down to the riot. Behind her, the wall. To the right, it was three car lengths to the roof of the neighboring building. And to the left, a ladder led up to the lookout platform on the fort wall.

With a crash, her makeshift barricade was overturned.

Nevada scrambled up the ladder. She emerged on the platform, where a Tuareg sniper sat patiently watching the riot below. He registered Nevada's presence and swung his rifle her way. Nevada threw the baton. It collided with his rifle, jarred it out of his hands, and sent it skittering off the edge of the platform.

"Not such a big man without your gun, are you?"

He stood up. It took a while, pulling out all six and a half feet between his shoelaces and his scalp.

"I take that back," Nevada said. "Still a big man. It's things like this that keep me humble."

He rushed at her, and Nevada barely touched the rungs as she plummeted back down the ladder, clearing his meaty hand just as it swiped at her hair. Below her, Nazir's men came onto the roof. There was no time to think, but then, Nevada had never been accused of being a great thinker. Holding onto the ladder, she kicked at the wall to catapult it the other way.

She rode the ladder down, dropping with a slow inevitability that made her wish for the dizzying vertigo falls were supposed to have. She couldn't even feel the wind passing by her. Then time unstuck so hard that it was like the world was shoving her downward. Air whistled by, her stomach climbed up into her throat, and the ground came at her until it didn't.

The ladder wedged itself between the two buildings, bridging the gap. Nevada hung down from the rungs, pulling air into lungs that momentarily couldn't believe they still needed it. Then she clambered up to stand on the makeshift tightrope and saw that on the rooftop she'd dropped down to, a Tuareg was waiting with *takoba* drawn.

"Seriously? With the sword? Are you the Highlander? Is there a Quickening in the area?"

He thrust the sword at her; she ducked backwards, barely catching herself on a rung of the horizontal ladder. He advanced with another slash.

Nevada retreated again. She chanced a look over her shoulder. Nazir's men were waiting for her with guns at the ready, not venturing onto the precarious ladder themselves but waiting for the swordsman to deliver her to them.

The swordsman carefully chose his footing and inched toward her, the sunlight blazing off his blade, making it pure light. His sword arm swung. Nevada dodged back a half second too slowly, and the tip of the blade carved a scarlet line across her belly. She winced in pain. A cheer went up from the Khamsin; the only thing better than killing Nevada would be taking her back to Nazir for flogging and other assorted character building. They jeered and booed as Nevada backed further down the ladder, only a step ahead of the swordsman's takoba.

And that step landed on a portion of the ladder that creaked threateningly under Nevada's weight, wood splintering. The swordsman froze. Nevada smiled.

"Fear of flying?" she asked and brought her foot down on the weak point as hard as she could.

The swordsman's face fell. Then the rest of him. The ladder shattered underneath them, breaking cleanly into two halves. As Nevada fell, she grabbed hold of the ladder. Reflex action. She'd been grabbing all her life, usually things that didn't belong to her, and it seemed the proper way to go out.

The ladder stopped suddenly, bringing her up short—its top rung hooked on the building's cornice so that its bottom rung, and Nevada with it, swung in a pendulum. Her arc carried her into a window. She burst through its wooden shutters, landed on her feet, and stumbled forward into what had to be Fedil's bedroom. Tasteless erotica on the walls, Persian rugs, and four Khamsin gunmen standing on a Kozak rug like they were waiting for her.

They weren't, and that was her only chance.

Instead of checking her stumble, Nevada kept her momentum going, breaking into a sprint. Nazir's men hadn't yet figured out who had lobbed a woman through the window, much less whether she would do the Dance of the Seven Veils or not. By the time she'd really registered, Nevada was almost on top of them.

One of them managed a snapshot. It went wide, stopping Nevada's heart for a moment before she flung herself into a baseball slide. Her heels dug into the carpet, jerking it out from under them. They went down while she came up.

She drove her knee into the nearest one's skull, cracking his head into the wall like she was making an omelet. Second one came to his feet. Nevada threw her forearm across his throat, knocked his Adam's apple into his spine. Third man came up swinging. She blocked with her left arm, threw out an uppercut with her right. Lifted his chin up, dislodged something in his neck—turned out he needed it. The fourth man was going for his gun. Nevada hurled herself at him and got her fist into his kidney. His knees buckled with the debilitating pain. Four hard rights to his face erased it and most of his features.

Nevada picked herself up. "Don't worry. Your old face was pretty worn out anyway."

One of them had been holding an FN SCAR. *Finally, a decent gun.* Nevada picked it up, checked the mag—*good enough for government work.* She barreled up the stairs and emerged onto the roof to see a ladder up to the wall-walk. Cracking gunshots forced her back inside. Nazir's men were firing at her from the opposite roof, keeping her pinned down until more of them worked their way up from the ground floor to corner her.

It finally happened. I'm finally in a position I can't fight or drink my way out of. Candice would've loved to see this.

She heard the chattering of helicopter blades chopping the air and saw the whirlybird itself pass overhead. Nazir. Not staying long enough to watch her die. Well, at least he wouldn't be able to give the show two thumbs-up either way.

The gunfire stopped—replaced by a cry of pain. Nevada heard something whistling through the air, an impact. Someone yelled, and Nevada saw a falling body pass by the window. Nazir's men were taking fire, having rocks and bits of broken masonry thrown at them by the slaves. They'd taken the courtyard, and now their aggression was turned on the remaining enemy.

The Khamsin gunmen tried to marshal a response, but Nevada cut them off. Switching the FN SCAR to full auto, she let them have everything in the clip. It wasn't the smoothest shooting she'd ever done, but then again, when taking a chainsaw to a bushel of wheat, there was no need for precision.

She looked down to the crowd and caught Savant in the throng. He gave her a thumbs-up. Nevada gave an OK sign back down to him and slung the rifle onto her shoulder. It was almost like she was having a good day.

From her high vantage point, she saw disaster coming before it hit. A phalanx of Tuaregs, reinforcements from some second location, came through the breached wall with twice the slaves' numbers. The slaves threw rocks, fired what few guns they had scavenged, but the Tuaregs' shields were locked in formation. The Tuaregs worked them to the far side of the fort with their advance, the thunder of their batons growing louder and louder. A couple of the slaves tried to throw themselves bodily against the juggernaut. They were smashed down by the shields and kept down by the electric sizzle of multiple stun batons. And there was nothing Nevada could do.

Nevada shot up the ladder to the top of the thickly crenellated wall and saw Jacques on the other side. He'd commandeered one of those limousines that looked like its father had been cuckolded by a Hummer.

"I know I'm a lesbian, but don't you think this is taking the butch thing a little far?" Nevada yelled down to him.

"It was this or camels!" Jacques yelled back. "No camels!"

"Did you at least kick the tires? All six of them?"

"What?"

"Never mind!" Nevada turned around, grabbing the ladder from the other side of the wall and hauling it up. It wouldn't cover all the distance, but it wasn't like a desert gave her a lot of options to break her fall with.

She stopped with the ladder in her hands. The slaves were cornered now. The guards pushed them against the wall, bringing their batons down mercilessly, not stopping until their victims fell.

"Fuck it," Nevada said, dropping the ladder. "Follow me!" she ordered Jacques

She took off the down the wall-walk.

Jacques cursed as he shifted the stretch Hummer into gear. "Peaudezébie! Where are you going?" he called up to her.

"To get myself killed!" Nevada shouted back, feeling optimistic.

Jacques stepped on the gas. "*Les femmes*—and they complain about us not asking for directions!"

Nevada ran around the wall, hearing sounds of violence rattle up from the courtyard as she circled. The guards laid into the slaves, not bothering to use their tasers anymore. They wanted to beat them into submission. Their batons pounded into flesh and splintered bone.

Nevada poured on speed like she was trying to see how loudly her aching body could complain. She rounded one corner, another, and came to the tower of Fedil's office. The shadow of the water tower fell over her, bringing a measure of cool relief as she gulped in air. Below her, Jacques's Hummer ground to a stop.

"Throw me the winch!" Nevada called down.

"What?"

"Front bumper! Winch! Throw it up! It'll be just like in Venezuela!"

Jacques slid out of his seat and rushed to the front bumper. He unspooled the tow hook, letting it dangle before he spun its weight around in a circle like a grappling hook. "Do you remember why we're not allowed in Venezuela anymore?"

Nevada held her hand down. "C'mon, c'mon!"

Jacques sent it flying. The tow hook almost reached the top of the wall before rebounding off the parapet, ricocheting out into the open air. Nevada shot her arm out to catch it, ended up wobbling on the very edge of the wall before righting herself. She threw the tow hook around one of the water tower's legs. It looped around it and caught on the line, forming an effective lasso. "Jacques, drive!"

The Hummer's engine revved beautifully as he backed up, drawing the line taut. Its loop dug into the old wood of the water tower's leg, which splintered, cracked. Nevada grinned.

"Going once." She ran the rifle over the line she'd anchored, turning the cable into a makeshift zipline. "Going twice."

Walking over the battlement, she dropped down into empty space, catching herself by her hold on the rifle. It slid down the line, carrying her from the top of the wall to the Hummer. She let go of the last few feet of the line, landed in a roll, and came up with her arm outstretched to catch herself against the Hummer's grille. Running over the hood and windshield, she swung into the passenger seat.

"Let's take our business elsewhere."

Jacques stood on the gas. The Hummer surged into motion, making the towing line cinch, then rip right through the leg of the water tower. The entire unbalanced tank toppled over, sending a tsunami cascading through the courtyard, making it a bad day to be carrying a stun baton.

"Well, that's my good deed for the day." Freed of its anchor, the towline retracted back into the winch. Jacques twisted the wheel, whirling them around to face away from the fort.

"I think you could stand some charity, though. Give me your jacket."

"It won't fit," Jacques warned her.

"How do you think my fist will fit in your eye?" Nevada reached over and took the wheel from him.

Jacques shrugged out of his jacket. "I think this is, how you say, buyer's remorse. *Au fait,* since I was here anyway, I picked you up something."

Nevada followed his gaze through the partition in back to see Fedil in the passenger area, bound and gagged. "Fedil! You're letting us borrow your ride? That is so sweet of you."

Every shudder of the helicopter's flight made Nazir's stump twinge, fresh pain firing up his arm and even out into the phantom fingers he could still feel moving. Made of nothing, feeling nothing. It was curious.

"We must get you to a doctor," Mahmoud said, pressing more cloth to the wound. "You're losing too much blood."

Nazir's attention was not on him. It was on the craft's radar. He remembered how the sweeping arm had painted the landscape upon their initial landing. Nothing but black. Now there was a splotch of green.

"What is that?" he asked the pilot, pointing with his one hand.

"Radar signature on the ground," the pilot explained. "We're only seeing it because we're so high up and the terrain is so flat."

"It wasn't there before."

The pilot clenched and unclenched his jaw. "Someone must've landed a plane there."

"Take me there now."

"My Khalifa," Mahmoud insisted, "we have no more men. And you need a doctor—"

Nazir grabbed him by the throat, but he spoke to the pilot. "You have flares onboard this craft?"

The pilot nodded.

Nazir turned to Mahmoud. "Cauterize."

Nevada scanned the dunes pressing in on all sides. She felt like she could be back home, a couple hundred years back, watching for Navajo lying in ambush. It didn't take much to imagine the grumbling jeep as a covered wagon, or the Sahara as a New Mexico wasteland. The great stillness around them, which swallowed up the jeep's many protesting noises, was big enough to encompass leagues and centuries alike.

Small wonder that she felt the need to speak up.

"Now that I've been a slave, it's really opened my eyes to social injustice, inequality, class warfare. You think I'll get anything if they give out reparations?"

Jacques scoffed. "*Sérieux*? It's called *Twelve Years a Slave*, not twelve minutes."

"Haven't you ever heard of a speed-run?" She grew serious. "Where's *The Flying Carpet*?"

"I set it down some miles from here. I thought it best to have it tucked out of the way of any festivities, knowing your penchant for *un dingue*."

Nevada looked over at the fuel gauge. "We have enough gas to get us there?"

"*Oui*, most assuredly. We are getting out of this *punaise*!" Jacques slapped the steering wheel for emphasis. "And the lovely Miss Cushing? Where is she?"

Nevada demurred, tilting her head back and forth. "Singh's got her. Went more douchebag than usual on us. We'll pick her up when we kick his ass. Save some fuel."

"*Tres bien*. Money…" Jacques began philosophically.

"Oh, here we go," Nevada muttered. "Is there a radio on this thing?"

"*Non*. Money is… necessary, it is important, but one cannot live for it. It is *bourgeoisie*." Jacques was starting to gesture. "Wine. Women. Art. These are the things of life."

"Had to lead with wine, didn't you?"

Jacques slapped her on the shoulder. "It's been a good few years. Very profitable. But that was work. This is *life*!"

"What are you talking about? We were trying to get the money for the kid, remember? That's not life?"

"*Je dis ça, je dis rien*. But there is a difference between providing for a child and being a mother. Just as there is a difference between saving our young damsel and…"

"And what?" Nevada interrupted. "I like her, okay? I admit it. I like Candice. And of course she's totally in love with me. But mostly I want to get revenge on Singh."

"*Ta gueule*."

"Don't underestimate the allure of revenge. They made four sequels to *Death Wish*, but *Sleepless in Seattle* was a one-off."

For all that he was usually in step with Nevada, when Jacques next spoke, it was with an unexpected somberness. "You're more used to being angry than being in love. But you'd be good at being in love. Take it from a Frenchman." He brightened. "Who would know better, *n'est-ce pas*?"

Nevada opened her mouth to protest, voice pitched to furious denial, but she couldn't find any words to fit into her objection. She ended up smiling lazily. "You may be right, Kermit. When was your last one-man wine tasting party? You're usually much less sober than this."

"Seeing as it is a special occasion, I have only drunken white wine."

"You know, in America we call that sparkling water."

Nevada checked the glove compartment and found a Ruger Speed-Six. She checked its cylinder, dry-fired it. It was in good shape. Probably would've brought more money than her at the auction. Pointing it out the window, she checked the sights. They looked as straight as the lesbian category on Pornhub.

The Sahara spread out in front of her gun barrel, golden brown sand forming sweeping dunes as smooth as glass, motionless save for the scree of loose sand that was drawn over them by the wind.

It made her think of Candice: mocha skin, honey-colored hair, the curves that made up her body. Nevada found herself treasuring the brief glimpses she had gotten of that body—soaked in sweat or awash in the crystalline water of an oasis—and recoiled mentally. You treasured people when they were gone. But she didn't know what to do with people who were still around. She'd save Candice, of course. And, by doing that, hand the woman incontrovertible proof that she cared. Deeply. Passionately. The way she'd always half-seriously tried to convince Candice she felt.

And so Nevada would be there, her heart on her sleeve and outside her bulletproof vest, and Candice would know exactly how she felt. She wondered what it would like—being the first one to say "I love you."

"*Merde*," Nevada muttered, making Jacques laugh.

"Yes, now we are riding the roller coaster, eh? Enough of the parlor games. Now we play for keeps!" He stood up on the gas pedal, bellowing with his fist in the air. "We fight for love!"

Nevada took the box of ammunition from the glove compartment and pocketed it in her jacket. "I hate Singh too, don't forget. So love and bitter resentment."

Forty minutes later, they were at *The Flying Carpet.* The air seethed, the sky was unbroken blue, and the sun turned it all gold like the fingertip of King Midas.

"You power the plane up," Nevada told Jacques. "I'll take care of Fedil."

Jacques hemmed a little.

"What?"

"I know he's a slave trader, *mon brave*, but killing him in cold blood seems a little... *déclassé*."

"You don't want me to kill him because it's *tacky*?"

"Yes, but I said it in French to be more sophisticated."

"Very convincing argument."

"One may not always have wealth or youth or beauty, but, " Jacques held up a finger, "one always has style."

"Fine. Cut him loose."

A moment later, Fedil was mouthing frantic thanks as Jacques ran the preflight checklist and Nevada retrieved the chocks.

"I swear to you, I swear, I will never do anything bad again! There will be no more slaves, there will be no more drugs—I will go to Mecca, that's what I will do. I will go to Mecca and Allah will show me the path!"

"Sounds like a long drive." Nevada tossed him the keys. "Speaking of which, while we were driving your car, me and Jacques noticed this weird engine noise? Sounded a little like, uh—"

Nevada drew her Ruger and fired five shots into the Hummer's radiator, leaving steam hissing in all directions.

"That," she concluded, replacing the gun in her waistband. "Might wanna get that checked out."

Jacques was powering the plane up when Nevada came up into the cockpit with the chocks slung over her shoulder. They clattered into the corner before she sat down in the copilot's seat.

"You know, in some countries that would still count as cold-blooded murder," Jacques said.

"Nah, I was pretty pissed off when I did it."

"Where to?"

"South Africa," Nevada said tiredly. Her eyelids were getting heavy. Through the windshield she saw nothing but little whirls of sand dancing for what few seconds they could before the wind died down. Nothing to hold her interest.

"That's where Singh is?"

Nevada rubbed at her eyes. "No, he wasn't kind enough to drop his itinerary. But Butch is there, and we need to talk to him."

"Butch? Your brother, Butch?"

"Who else but my parents would name someone Butch in this day and age? If anyone knows where Singh is going, it's him. He was born with his ear to the ground. It was pretty unsanitary, but our folks saved a bunch of money."

Jacques occupied himself with ignoring Fedil as he screamed obscenities at them from outside. "And you are on speaking terms with him at the present time?"

"He's family. Why wouldn't I be?"

"You two always run hot and cold. When was the last time you spoke?"

"I don't know—Thanksgiving?" Nevada ventured. "Just fly the plane, dude. *Rompez*!"

Jacques started the props spinning. "It's four thousand miles to South Africa. Two days in the air. We'll need to refuel."

Nevada leaned her head back, eyes closing. "I'll spring for gas if you pay for chips."

Jacques reached between their seats, opening the hatch that led into the nose compartment, where he'd replaced the pimply radome on the nose with a Plexiglass viewport. It was an excellent place to stow a cooler. He opened one up, brought out a bottled water, and pressed it into Nevada's arms. "Here. Rehydrate. Then go in back and sleep there. You know what sleeping in one of these chairs does to your back."

Nevada puffed out her cheeks. "How bad can it be if I'm so comfortable?"

"Besides, you snore."

Nevada punched him in the shoulder as she got up. "Lies. Blatant lies. I'm sleeping in the nose."

Grabbing up a bedroll, Nevada went down the few stairs that led below the cockpit. She situated herself above the landing gear and went to sleep watching the horizon prowl towards her, hoping it was bringing Candice closer and closer.

CHAPTER 4

Candice Cushing thought hard. With a bag over her head and her hands cuffed behind her back, there was little else she could do. Even if she could memorize how often the jeep she was in went over a pothole or how long they went without stopping, she couldn't see any point in retracing their route. She hadn't known where she was when they'd kidnapped her.

She thought of Rudolf Carl von Slatin, the Austrian soldier who'd become governor general, or Bey, of Darfur under Charles George Gordon. In the Mahdist War, his Muslim troops were being defeated, demoralized by fighting under an infidel. In answer, Slatin had publicly converted to Islam, spurring his army on, but not enough to defeat the Mahdi. After gamely prolonging the inevitable, he'd surrendered and was taken to the Mahdi's encampment, where he was treated as a guest. He wrote to Gordon, explaining his actions and asking for permission to escape.

Gordon refused. Slatin turning his back on Christianity could not be forgiven.

Candice wondered what her own apostasy was. She'd made a deal with Easy Nevada, agreeing to give up one small part of the find Nevada had promised to help her uncover, and justified it to herself by saying that it was worth it to get the rest of the archaeological treasure trove. And maybe if she'd remained objective, then it wouldn't have been *so* bad. Except she'd developed feelings for Nevada. How deep and how real and if Nevada truly returned them, she couldn't say. But here she was, trying to think of the Bey of Darfur and not…

There was a horrible joke in there somewhere, but without Nevada she didn't have to worry too much about finding it.

The Bey of Darfur and not *the bae.* Candice smiled under her hood. Awful. Terrible. If Nevada rescued her, she'd inflict that one on her first chance she got. *So what's taking you so bloody long, Thea?*

All at once, light burst into her private world. She tried blinking it away and failed but grew used to the brightness after a few moments. She was in the back of a Land Rover. Through the windows she saw the standardized monotony of yellow sand and blue sky that she'd long since become used to, dust devils stinging at the ground and then pulling away like it was an animal they could wound but not kill. And sitting across from her was John Gore, wiping his black hands on a handkerchief.

"Handcuffs are for stupid people. Do you need the handcuffs?"

Candice shook her head. He held up the key and she wiggled over onto her hip, presenting her hands. Gore unlocked the cuffs, brought her hands around in front of her, and clicked the cuffs shut again.

"Trust is overrated," he explained. "But it hardly matters if you see someone's face or know where we're going. So why not make you comfortable?"

Candice ignored the implications of that. There were too many flutters in her stomach already. "Where are we going?"

"Plane," he said simply.

"Where's the plane going?"

"Up," he answered. "You want a cigarette?"

"No."

"Water?"

"Yes. Please."

Gore stooped down. Wedged under his seat was a 24-pack of bottled water. He tugged one of the bottles free of the plastic wrap and pressed it insistently into her cuffed hands. Candice got the message: *Don't try to use this as a weapon.* Candice didn't know whether to be flattered he thought she could do any damage with it or insulted he thought she was stupid enough to try.

"Why bother with the hood in the first place?" Candice asked after a lengthy drink that tasted stingingly of iodine purification.

Gore shrugged. "Probably because the boss saw it in a movie once."

Candice looked at him, fuming with anger over his nonchalance. So easy to be cool when she was in handcuffs. "You know, whatever his plan is, it's not going to work."

Gore dug into his pocket for a pack of cigarettes. "What makes you say that?"

"He's an idiot."

Gore conceded the point with a slight inclination of his head. He lit his chosen cigarette. "'The reasonable man adapts himself to the world: the unreasonable one persists in trying to adapt the world to himself. Therefore all progress depends on the unreasonable man.'"

"That's what you think he's doing? Progress?"

Gore was saturnine, his voice as featureless as some mass-produced product off an assembly line. "I think unreasonable men get lucky. Especially unreasonable men with lots of money. And if they don't, their checks still clear."

"So this is all just a payday for you?"

Gore pulled deeply on his cigarette. "How much does an archaeologist make in a year?"

"I don't kill people."

"If you do, it's a highly marketable skill." Gore smiled around his cigarette. "Guess we're at an impasse. You don't need to go to the bathroom or anything like that, do you?"

"No."

"Shame. These drives get kinda boring."

He's trying to psyche you out, Candice thought. *The more cowed you are, the better a prisoner you are. Don't give him an inch.* Out loud, she asked, "You ever watch *Bewitched*?"

Gore took another drag on his cigarette; the black sweat of his fingertips left an oily stain on the rolling paper. "Can't say that I have."

"The male lead, Darrin? The guy married to the witch? They replaced him. Got an entirely different actor to play the role. How do you think it felt, being the second choice?"

Gore let the cigarette dangle from his lower lip as he wiped his hands on the handkerchief again. "I admit it, I'm stumped. Your dry British wit is too much for me. What the hell are you talking about?"

"Singh set Nevada after the skulls first. You were the runner-up. And the number-one draft pick is coming to kill you."

Gore took the cigarette between his fingers again. "Nevada's bones are bleaching in the desert by now."

Candice smiled at him. "She found a boat... in the middle of the Sahara... *and she sank it.*" She leaned back in her seat. "She's coming for me. With a highly marketable skill."

Gore filled his lungs with smoke again. "I'm starting to see the point of the hood."

The Land Rover pulled to a halt. Gore took Candice by the elbow, leading her out of the jeep with the tired expertise of a slaughterhouse worker near the end of shift. Outside, an airstrip shone through the sand like scalp through the hair of a balding man. A frame cabin on top of a rusting derrick served as air traffic control, while hangars provided shelter for planes, crews, and cargo. Abandoned pallets littered the sides of the runway. Sand drifted over the pitted tarmac in a half-hearted attempt to hide it from view.

Alone in all the dereliction was a private jet. It looked as if someone had taken a yacht and pared it down until a set of wings could carry it. Gore kept her moving lockstep toward it, his hand on her shoulder as solid as a ball and chain.

She ascended the stairs and Gore finally let go of her. He left a black handprint on her shoulder. His body crowded into the doorway behind Candice, blocking it off, but she didn't think she had the willpower to pull herself away from the air conditioning and gentle lighting of the plane's interior. It was heaven.

Gore gave her a shove. Her legs suddenly wouldn't carry her. She stumbled her way into one of the chairs—not in rows, not cramped, not hard—and sank down. Candice wouldn't have thought she'd be so ready to sit down after the hours of driving. But there was sitting, and then there was *sitting*.

"Yeah. That's good. Have a seat." Singh's prissy voice spoiled the moment.

Candice forced her relaxed eyes open. He'd changed into another floridly preening suit. She didn't know if he was pretentious enough to wear more than one suit a day or if an entire twenty-four hours had passed since she'd last seen him. Maybe both.

"Can I get something to eat?" Candice asked. "Nothing much. Two, three courses max."

Gore smirked. "You sound like her. Your good friend Easy Nevada is rubbing off on you."

"Phrasing," Candice said warningly.

"Ugh!" Singh heaved a sigh as he ran his hands through his hair. "You're so good at this, John. You're threatening *and* cool. It's so money."

Gore accepted the praise by way of clearing his throat.

"I can't live up to that," Singh admitted to Candice casually, as though they were exchanging gossip. "I mean, he lives to be intimidating. It's his job to be intimidating. So I'll talk and you just chime in whenever. And if we need to terrorize you, I'll let him do that. You don't mind, do you, John?"

Gore took a last puff on his cigarette before pitching it out onto the runway. "It's a living."

"Now, Candice, I don't know how you're holding up—maybe you have posttraumatic stress disorder—"

"What's post about my trauma?" Candice interrupted.

Singh sprawled in his seat, one leg over the armrest. "Oh, RSVP the pity party, babe. There's air-conditioning. There's wine spritzers. A lot of hostages would love to be in your shoes right now. John, you didn't rape her or anything, right?"

"No."

Singh gestured placidly to Candice. "Okay, good. So no trauma, no regressing to childhood, we're all on the same page. Candice—"

"Dr. Cushing."

Singh glanced at Gore. "Is she?" He looked back at Candice without waiting for a reply. "You're not a doctor-doctor, okay, so who cares? *Candice*, you remember finding the last of the twelve crystal skulls I've been paying your friend Nevada to get me, yeah?"

"It rings a bell."

"Good. And it lit up, yes? It lit up?" Singh nodded—nodded at Gore, nodded at Candice.

She gave a hesitant nod.

"Yes!" He leapt on her affirmation. "It glowed. Shined. Whatever." He clapped his hands. "So this is real simple. You tell us what you did to make it do that. Once we get it working, we let you go. Otherwise…" Singh paused, then snapped his fingers. "John, what's a good—like a good torture kinda?"

"Just leave it implied," Gore told him.

"Okay, cool, we're just implying it for now." Singh shifted in his seat. "But the thing we're implying is torture. John, you know torture, right?"

Gore shrugged. "It's pretty simple. You cut off some fingers, pull out some teeth. They'll talk before you're done."

Singh's face twisted. "Hey, whoa, keep that to yourself, guy. I haven't eaten yet! God, no wonder you imply this stuff! That's gross!"

"So you're not going to do it?" Candice asked tiredly.

"Me, no. Him, absolutely. It's called delegating. It's a managerial technique. So," Singh spread his hands wide, "lay it on me."

"I don't know how or why the skull did anything. And if I did know, I certainly wouldn't tell you." Candice sneered. "Even if it's just a glorified torch, that's more power than you should have, you jumped-up tosspot."

Singh's jaw dropped for a moment, then he glared at Gore. "See? I told you we shouldn't have just implied stuff." To Candice he said, "Hey, idiot, you're going to be tortured! How long do you think you can take being tortured?"

"Longer than you can watch, I'll wager."

Singh bit his lip in consideration. "We're not so different, you and I."

Candice frowned. "Yes we are. We're totally different."

"I know. I just always wanted to say that."

His hand on his earpiece, Gore crossed the cabin to stoop and whisper in Singh's ear. Singh smiled.

"Oh? Now? Good, go get it. Bring it out. Shoo!" Singh cuffed Gore lightly on the back as he moved to the back of the plane. Then he directed his smile at Candice. She felt like she'd found a roach in a silverware drawer.

"Actually, I think you are going to help me. In fact, I think you're going to beg to help me," he said

Gore came back and handed over a laptop. Singh took it from him like a child accepting a lolly.

"You're going to take one look at this," he said, "and then you won't have any choice."

CHAPTER 5

Johnnie Walker flowed into the Old Fashioned glass in a languid caress, followed by the mischievous *plop* of an ice ball sinking under the surface. The two inches of ice cracked slightly as they came to a rest, and Nevada's eyes did the same. She took in the light froth of pearl-fine bubbles that danced along the curvature of the ice before swirling out into the surrounding amber.

"I thought that might wake you up," Jacques said cheerfully, shaking the glass so the ice chimed off its interior.

It probably wasn't morning, but that didn't make dealing with a morning person any easier.

"You've finally learned something about women. It only took the better part of a decade."

"On the rocks," Jacques said, handing her the glass. "One must always stay on brand."

Nevada downed the whiskey in one go. Whatever else she felt, it wasn't bleary. "Since you're not flying the plane, I take it we've landed?"

"That, or I'm getting forgetful in my old age." Jacques sat down on the stairs. "You've been asleep all day. I, on the other hand, have had coffee."

"So where are we?"

"South Africa," Jacques answered, taking the empty glass back. "Just inside the border. We were running on fumes. But with a full tank of gas and a few more hours' flight—I wasn't able to get hold of Butch, but I did find he has land holdings in a province I will not try to pronounce. There's an airstrip nearby. We may find him there."

"Land holdings?" Nevada asked. "Since when has Butch been a land holdings kind of guy?"

"You never know. Even South Africa must have strip malls."

"Don't be mean," Nevada chided him. "How long until we're wheels up again?"

"Not long now. But I have taken the liberty of slipping a porter twenty dollars. You can use the airport locker room if you wish to wash up."

"What would I do without you, Jacques?"

"Your own laundry."

The airstrip was the horse in a one-horse town. There were some shops and office buildings of Western design, as well as rondavels—round mud huts under thatched roofs. The mishmash looked a little gruesome to Nevada, like charming Swedish cottages next door to the bluntness of fast-food joints and Starbucks. She gathered up what fresh clothes she could from a nearly depleted inventory and wrapped the Ruger inside the bundle. Jacques's directions led her off the airfield, through a baggage claim with nothing to claim, and into a locker room. A quick search turned up no soap, so she settled for scouring herself under the hot water, her gun in the soap dish to discourage guests.

It was possible, Nevada thought, that her life had gotten off track since she was eleven and wanted to own all the horses in the world.

After she'd given the water a fair shot at returning her to a state of grace, she dressed in the few clothes she'd found that could match her in cleanliness. Nevada had long since gotten into the habit of keeping fresh underwear still in the package for occasions like this, and to that she added jeans that had surely only been worn a day since their last visit to a washing machine and a T-shirt with the slogan *Hands Off My Tuts* and two of the iconic funerary masks in obvious locations. It had been meant to be a gag gift.

Dressed, Nevada strolled out into the tiny airport's concourse, which proved to be something like an outlet mall version of the usual *Twilight Zone*. She bought a Shangaan bag to deposit her old clothes in and Chinese food, both signs of the growing Sino-African hierarchy. America was firing its own barrages—she ate her food under a mosaic of Steve Biko that was being replaced by a mural of the Black Panther, trademark sign in the lower right.

Back outside, the sun poured down heat, making the runway sizzle under Nevada's shoes. To her frazzled nerves, the heat seemed much the same as the Sahara, only more humid. She thrust herself into *The Flying Carpet*'s air-conditioned interior, pausing to look up at the powder puff cumulus clouds frying up in the African sky like snow falling in reverse.

I'm not usually so uncharitable, she thought, doing her half of the plane's preflight chores. Her attitude was that there wasn't much point in world travel if you couldn't enjoy it and not get bogged down in the odd dead body. Candice's kidnapping had gotten to her. Or maybe she was starting her period.

She took up the copilot's seat with a tube of lipstick in hand—Revlon Super Lustrous in Rich Girl Red—which she used to cheat her face of looking like she'd made no effort whatsoever.

"I haven't put makeup on in almost a week. I'm starting to worry this is what I really look like."

Jacques busied himself over the controls. "I thought lesbians didn't care about makeup."

"Men do!" Nevada protested, barely audible as the two Curtiss-Wright R-1820 engines cleared their throats, the propellers churning into motion, all of it sounding like some fat jazz singer coming to the stage with his baritone voice lugged around in his chest.

Jacques reached up to the overhead panel, grabbing a fistful of throttle and easing it up. "Why do you care if men are attracted to you?"

"Men want to fuck cars! Do you realize how demeaning it is to have them not want to fuck you?"

"I don't want to fuck you," Jacques pointed out.

"You take that back."

The engines reached a fever pitch. Jacques pulled back on the yoke, bringing them up as smoothly as an elevator.

They had been friends for so long that uncomfortable silence had been eliminated from their repertoire. Nevada happily left Jacques to his own thoughts as she leaned back and let the plane's vibration massage her taut body. It didn't relieve her tension so much as polish it to a fine sheen. Every mile was another mile closer to Candice—she hoped.

At first, the clouds they passed were the same wisps Nevada had seen at the airport. Scraps of moisture ripped apart by drought. But as the hours passed, the clouds grew like Towers of Babel, becoming lightning-toothed mountains that Jacques carefully circumvented. *The Flying Carpet* dipped under the clouds' pregnant bellies, almost caressing them, until suddenly rain was dotting the windshield and dappling the skin of the plane. Nevada put her hand on the window glass to feel the damp cool of the outside, the smell slipping into *The Flying Carpet* with a freshness that was almost intoxicating.

She glanced at Jacques, trying to share a smile, but in the cockpit, he was all business. "It's virga," he said. "It'll evaporate before it hits the ground."

Nevada felt a swell of emotion at that. Her equilibrium was not proving to be as invulnerable as usual. In stray moments, she thought of Candice being held prisoner—it was like touching a live wire. She'd been around too long to believe there was any gentleman's agreement when it came to the bad guys of the world. Nevada had been lucky enough to make it through her own close calls with only a few scars, all on the outside. And as comfortable as she was with gambling her own life, the thought that Candice might be dead already…

"I've been thinking about what you said."

"But of course," Jacques replied. "My sayings are very memorable."

Nevada rolled her eyes mildly but was otherwise as tender as a lamb. "It's… I don't know. It's kinda hard to sort out. I can't have Candice's death on my conscience. I just can't. But, what, that means I actually want her in my life? With her stupid face, like, all the time? I mean, she's not into me, so she's clearly crazy, and that's not good for a relationship, but she did agree to go out with me, but that could've been because I saved her life, which I've done a lot, by the way, so don't think I feel obligated this time, I just… It's very classy. I'm a very classy lady and I do stuff, like recycling and saving damsels in distress. Which is another way I'm freaking great, so maybe she is in love with me. She could also feel obligated, so between those two things, I think I can talk her into some pretty freaky stuff."

"It's easy to tell you don't care very much when you've clearly put so little thought into it."

"Yeah, exactly. Wait…" Nevada blinked. "*Ta gueule*! Jerk."

"And when you clearly aren't emotionally invested at all," Jacques needled.

"I'm *used* to her, okay?" Nevada said defensively. "She's my Candice, and I can't have people beating up my Candice!"

Jacques laughed and shook his head in the time it took for Nevada to realize what she'd said. "If this *beau sabreur* cares for you as much as you care for her, I may safely retire," he responded.

Now it was Nevada's turn to guffaw. "What are you talking about, old man? When they haul this thing to the scrapheap, you're still going to be in the pilot's seat. They're going to have to wheel you out."

Jacques laughed too, but humorlessly. "You have it exactly. 'Old man.' I feel it coming over me like *le cafard*. I won't be able to protect you much longer. And you don't need me to."

"Bullshit. I needed you back in the desert, didn't I?"

Jacques smiled, making a crater in his face of wrinkles and laugh lines and the white hair of his stubble. "*Mauvais sujet*, you have spent your life climbing through ruins and digging up bones, but you haven't learned the most important thing they have to teach."

"Oh yeah? What's that?"

"Nothing lasts forever."

It wasn't Jacques who had spoken. It was a voice, male and familiar, coming from behind them. Nevada spun in her seat and found herself looking down the barrel of a gun. So close she could see the bullet slotted into the chamber as it was cocked.

"Hello again," Nazir said.

CHAPTER 6

Singh opened the laptop in front of Candice, showing her a black screen reflecting herself and the spacious cabin of the Gulfstream jet, with a log-in prompt hanging in the middle.

"You have to log in," Candice said.

"What?" Singh turned the laptop around to read it himself.

"It logged you out," Candice continued.

"I set it not to log me out," Singh said, typing in his password. "Why would it need to log me out? I'm the only one that uses it." He hit Enter. "It's not taking my password."

"Do you have the Caps Lock on?" Candice asked. "Usually it's the Caps Lock."

"I'm trying it," Singh insisted, before looking over his shoulder at Gore. "Gore, I want you to set my computer so it doesn't log me out, okay?" He pressed Enter again. "Here, now it's working."

He spun the laptop around to face Candice again. She saw graying mountains of clouds, lightning sizzling inside the dark vapor, the viewpoint high above the patchwork terrain of towns, jungle, grass. Near the center was *The Flying Carpet*'s ungainly bulk, the flying boat chugging away with all the grace of its name, as seen by the camera of some sort of drone.

"Just one word and I can shoot her out of the sky," Singh said. Candice almost asked which he meant: the plane or Nevada?

"You're bluffing," she said instinctively—some tumor of Nevada had gotten into her, saying what she would've said, which only made Candice more heartsick. This would be so much easier with Nevada here, being strong, so that all Candice had to do was be smart. Always so easy being smart, especially when there wasn't a gun being waved around. "What do you want?"

Singh smirked. Candice guessed the first part of it was that: having her treat him like a Bond villain again after he'd been all Boomer with the laptop. "I told you. Get the skull to work."

"I can't. I don't know how. *I told you*," Candice insisted.

"I don't believe you," Singh said. "Gore!"

Gore was on the phone. He gave a sharp nod and spoke in a low voice, his free hand blocking his other ear.

Singh looked out the expansive window between himself and Candice. Almost helplessly, Candice followed his gaze to the curvature of the earth and the never-ending sprawl of cities and mountains reduced to models. He didn't look impressed or awed. It was like he was bored by the vista, utterly used to it.

"I'll admit it, I'm not the smartest guy in the room," Singh said with the faux confessional tone of a used-car salesman.

"Plane," Candice corrected automatically.

Singh barreled on. "I don't know books or term papers, but I don't have to. I know people, and people are the ones who read books, and who write most of them too. So I know your type. The gifted child. I bet people expected great things from you since kindergarten."

"People expected me to work hard since kindergarten," Candice replied. "There's a difference."

"Well, no one expected anything of me. My father was rich, family was rich—I was just supposed to leave cruise control on. When I went to school, I got my tests handed out with the answers already filled in."

"And you resented it."

Singh shook his head in a flurry of motion. "No, I loved it. Who wouldn't? No one gets this, but there's a roadmap to these things. It's very *Henry V*," he said, pronouncing the five as "vee." "You party in high school, college, it shows you're well-adjusted. Then you party in yachts, at Cannes—shows you're prosperous. If you have money, then you're making money, so the company is making money. The hotter the escorts, the better your stock price. People don't get that."

"Fine. Drop me off at the next boat show, and get back to Little St. James Island."

Singh wagged his finger at her. "All those As and you still don't get it. The free ride's ending. Dubai is built on oil, four billion barrels of it, but they're running out. When that's gone, all that's left is a party being thrown in the desert with no refreshments."

"So go green," she countered.

Singh blew air through pursed lips. "No-go. None of those technologies are as good as nuclear, and no one wants nuclear because they're scared of it. I think it's the impotence thing. People get real weird about being impotent. So what I need is a new technology. Something that will make Dubai prosperous forever, and then you, my father, everyone who ever dismissed me will see that I had a vision all along. You'll all see. But first, you have to make my skull work."

Candice hiccupped a laugh. "You're going to replace the internal-combustion engine with a glowing skull?"

Singh threw up his shoulders in a shrug. "Fine. Don't believe me—doubt away. Just make the skull work and I can be nice to you. I like being nice. I'm a good guy!"

"I told you, I don't know how."

Singh took a deep breath. "I *know people*," he stressed. "Nevada's in love with you, and she's too much of a mercenary to do anything without getting something out of it, so you must be in love with her too. Work the skull, or watch her die."

Candice tried to make herself do it. Nevada had said that the skulls were no more than knick-knacks, and she had no reason to believe differently. Singh thought they were the next stage in human evolution, which was reason enough to think they were no more special than the Baghdad Battery—or Piltdown Man. And as tempting as it was to defy Singh out of sheer spite, helping him with some meaningless pet project was probably her best chance to get out of this alive, to say nothing of saving Nevada, if Singh could attack her as he claimed.

But she couldn't shake the sense of foreboding she'd felt in Cleopatra's tomb when the damn thing had lit up. Every bit of her that was rational could only think that it was a clever trick, at most a curiosity—yet it had seemed so profound. It still did.

She was an archaeologist. The modern world often seemed thin and insubstantial to her, whereas history was solid, heavy, even crushing. An Etruscan vase had heft to it that no iPhone could. And the skull had blown away every other artifact she'd ever seen. The weight of years behind it was so vast, it was overwhelming. Whatever that power was, she didn't trust Singh with it. She didn't know if anyone *could* be trusted with it.

But thin, insubstantial modernity was her world, even if it disappointed her. In all the centuries, on every continent, among every people, there was only one Easy Nevada. Candice didn't know if there was any higher meaning to them coexisting, meeting, even developing feelings for one another, but there was only one of her. That made her rarer than twelve crystal skulls.

Gore cupped the phone to his chest. "We're ready."

Singh looked at Candice expectantly. "Well?"

He knows people. But he doesn't know me.

"You're bluffing." She willed the thought into existence, bent the universe to make it so. No matter what, *he was bluffing.*

Singh cocked his head, not looking disappointed in the slightest. Candice realized he wasn't. As much as he wanted her to give in to him, he was just as happy to be given an excuse to—break her.

My God, he really is mad.

"Fire," Singh said without looking away. Gore muttered into the phone, and a moment later, under Singh's watchful eye, Candice saw on the laptop how a missile streaked out from under the camera and screamed toward *The Flying Carpet.*

CHAPTER 7

Under the crushing muteness of her headphones, Nevada heard the steady drone of the radial engines, monastic chanting in this flying cathedral. It went hand in hand with the vibration that pulsed through the great bulk of the Grumman Albatross, the sheer power that was keeping it airborne bleeding into a vibrant shake that had become reassuring after all these years in the sky. The gun in Nazir's hand shook, but that was only the engines. The hatred in his eyes didn't quiver at all.

Nevada glanced at Jacques. "Hey, bro, you order a one-handed Arab guy? Because I could've gotten one with two hands at the gift shop if you wanted one that bad."

"Up!" Nazir ordered, gesturing with the gun and shouting to be heard over the props.

Nevada got up, taking off her headphones and letting in the overpowering roar of the engines. Out of her seat and not strapped in, the vibrations of the plane buzzed at her feet. Only long-developed sea legs kept her from losing her footing. Nazir had the elbow of his other arm against the hatch for stability.

She looked at the passenger seats behind the pilot and copilot's stations. The Shangaan bag she'd picked up at the airport was behind Jacques. In it, she'd stowed the dirty clothes she'd taken off before her shower and the gun she'd taken for protection.

Of course, even an idiot like Nazir would shoot her if she started rooting through a bag all of a sudden.

Nevada steadied herself, resting both hands on the seats in back, the bag and the gun only a foot away from her right hand. "I gotta hand it to you, Wiz. I have no idea how you caught up with us."

"I've been ahead of you," Nazir said. "I found your plane from the air and hid myself inside to await you. Unfortunately, I lost consciousness shortly after." He held up his bandaged stump. "Even Allah only gives his servants so much strength. But now I have strength enough to attend to our business. And your friend can't intercede as before; not while he flies the plane."

"So you think just because Jacques is flying the plane that he's gonna knuckle under?" Nevada asked as a bout of turbulence stole her stability. She jolted down, her hand slipping closer to the bag—its handle brushing against her wrist—but she forced herself to bring her hand back up, tightening her fingers on the shoulder of the seat. Nazir was still on edge. She wouldn't get anything past him while his doll eyes were watching her so closely.

Nazir's thumb stroked the gun in his hand. "You can't goad me with your jokes. You won't get a quick death no matter what you say. No, I have a slow death in mind for you—and many bullets in this gun. I wonder where the first should go. Where to hurt you before you go into shock."

"Don't ask me. When it comes to torture, I'm all thumbs."

Nazir cocked the gun like he was ready to use it then and there.

"If you shoot her," Jacques said firmly, "I will crash this plane."

Nazir let out a disbelieving laugh. "I know martyrs, *monsieur*. You are not one."

Jacques took his hands off the yoke.

It had to be her imagination, but Nevada thought she could hear a shift in the pitch of the engines, something slow and subtle changing in its sound as the plane began to drift off course.

Nazir shook the gun at him. "Control the plane once more!"

"And what will you do otherwise?" Jacques asked. "Shoot me?"

Nazir aimed at Nevada.

"Hey, I'm as stumped as you are," she said.

Nazir's eyes went dark, considering the problem, and Nevada's fingertips tingled with their closeness to the gun. Now, when he was distracted, turning over his options—but it seemed too soon, too quick. An ineffable sense of danger warned Nevada away from chancing it now. Her hand still burned. She knew exactly how it would fit around the butt of the gun, how the trigger would feel against the pad of her forefinger…

Nazir nodded to himself. "Yes, yes, I can land the plane myself…"

"Best of luck, monsieur," Jacques said with perfect deadpan. "We are an hour out from landing, and you don't even know what direction to go in."

Nevada bit back her own reply, something about how she was sure most airlines used on-the-job training when it came to their pilots or maybe something about wrists, if she could come up with a pun. The less attention Nazir paid to her, the better. With all his focus on Jacques, she might just have enough time to draw and fire before he could react.

Nazir seized on a new plan, excitement crowning in his voice. "Then I'll shoot both of you and help myself to a parachute."

"*Zut*, you have outmaneuvered us, then. Assuming you know where they are—can find them before we crash?"

With a growl, Nazir spun Nevada around and wrapped his amputated arm around her throat. It happened so quickly that Nevada's hand was left tangled in the Shangaan bag's handle, the weight of the gun inside dangling from her wrist.

"Then we're going looking for them," Nazir spat, holding his gun to her head. "That will give Easy and I plenty of time to get to know each other."

He shoved her from the flight deck into the passenger compartment. Her Shangaan bag smacked against the side of the hatch with a metallic clang. Nazir froze. His gun grew enormous in her vision as she turned to face him.

"What was that?" he demanded.

"What was what?" Nevada replied. "This?" She raised the purse in her right hand. "Or this?" She brought up her left hand while directing her gaze on it, the flicker of motion and Nevada's own shifting attention pulling Nazir's focus to it like she was dragging on a rope. In that momentary diversion, she swung the purse like a flail, slamming the weight of the gun inside into Nazir's temple.

He tripped to the side, his gun going off—Nevada felt the heat of the muzzle flash across her midsection, heard the bullet pinging through the flight deck in ricochet after ricochet, but by then she'd already barreled into Nazir. She crushed him to the ground underneath her, fist already cocked to piston down into his face, smashing it into the deck. He tried to bring up the gun in his hand; Nevada caught his wrist in her other hand and slammed it down. The gun jolted out of his fingers. She jammed another punch into his face, and a spasm shook his body.

"Getting to know me yet?" Nevada hissed down at him, bringing her fist up for more when the wing of *The Flying Carpet* exploded.

The force of the blast traveled right through the plane's fuselage, a shockwave picking Nevada up and dashing her against the wall. Her head thudded against metal that wasn't about to give, and she came down in a heap, seeing colors bursting in front of her eyes, painful in their intensity. Darkness called out to her, cool and sweet, but she ignored it like a three-inch dick pic.

Holding onto consciousness by her teeth, Nevada fought her way to her feet, only for Nazir to charge into her, shoulder digging into her midsection. Conjoined, they plunged back into the flight deck, Nazir driving her into the console between the pilot and copilot's seats. Nevada had a brief glimpse of Jacques clutching his stomach before the console gave way, catapulting her and Nazir down into the bow compartment.

Nevada landed below the Plexiglass nose dome and took in the view it offered straight ahead, precariously tilting downwards as the plane went into a nosedive. Nazir was oblivious to it. He pinned her down with his bulk, forearm cutting into her throat, squeezing the air out of her. Nevada looked up at him: jaw hanging brokenly off his face, features covered in blood, eyes blazing with hatred. His broken mouth gurgled with nonsense words, Arabic drowned in bubbling blood. It must have been killing him to speak, but adrenaline made him determined to be heard.

Nevada reached past him, touching the clasp overhead. The compartment's hatch unlocked In a heartbeat, it was ripped open by the wind rushing by the plane. Nazir was suddenly exposed to the wind at twenty thousand feet up. It whirled around him, ripped at his clothes, froze his flesh. And while he was distracted, Nevada went for the hat trick, plowing her fist into his face again and reducing his nose to the same condition as his jaw. He let go of her, clutching protectively at his destroyed face. Nevada shoved her palms into his chest, shoving him far enough up for her to get her knees in between them, legs coiled, feet against his gut.

"Sorry, sir, but I have to downgrade your seat assignment," she chirped in her best flight attendant voice before kicking out with both legs as hard as she could.

Nazir flew straight up, outside the protection of the bow compartment—didn't even have time to scream before the slipstream hit him and tore him far away from *The Flying Carpet.*

Nevada grabbed the hatch's handles and wrenched them inward, fighting the rush of air to lock the hatch back into place before she emerged up onto the flight deck.

She collapsed into the copilot's seat. "He had a decent plan, but as it turned out, he just wasn't well-armed."

"Sorry I couldn't help," Jacques said, his voice reedy.

"That's okay. One of us needs to look pretty for the cameras."

"Besides," Jacques wheezed, his breath leaking out instead of animating his words, "you've never needed much in the way of help."

Nevada looked at him. Saw the charred hole in his shirt's midsection, under the breast, bright red spilling out to swallow up the taupe fabric. Panic flared in her, dismay, every emotion that could curdle innards, but most of all she felt a nauseously slick feeling of guilt as she detached from those emotions. Nevada ripped her left sleeve off, stuffed it against the wound, and then rearranged one of the seatbelts so that it pulled taut on the makeshift bandage, put pressure on it for her. Blood wetting her hands, she attended to the controls. *The Flying Carpet* still nosed down, filling its windshield with trees, and her strong pull on the yoke only slightly changed their trajectory.

Nevada tried to ignore a droning hum as the plane knifed through the air, picking up speed, screaming for the ground. "What's wrong with this crate?"

"We were hit by a missile," Jacques said, his voice so weak that Nevada wanted to let go of the controls and look him over again.

"So?" Nevada demanded, glancing over at him and seeing through the window that the right propeller was only half there, the blades moving spasmodically, but the radial engine that had powered them had been bitten clean off by the explosion. "Okay—how many wings does a plane really need? Like, *really*?"

"Get to the parachutes," Jacques told her. He reached for the yoke. "I can hold her steady long enough."

"You're in no condition to go skydiving."

"I know I'm not," Jacques said gently. Nevada looked at him. He was smiling—trying to be reassuring—blood on his teeth. "They're going to have to wheel me out, remember?"

Nevada shook her head. "No. Fuck that. How far to the landing strip?"

"Forty minutes. Easy—"

"So we'll land..." Nevada dragged the yoke back, veins standing out on her arms as she muscled it as far back as it would go. Her eyes blazed even harder, like she would rip the yoke out if she had to, like she could keep the plane up with sheer will. "We'll get you help. Just talk me through it. I've seen you do this a thousand times."

Jacques cleared his throat and spat to the side. Nevada didn't look to see what color it was. "Open up the throttle. We have to build up lift if we want to pull up."

Nevada reached up to grasp the throttle and wrench it forward. "See? Nothing to it. Now, how hard can landing be?"

CHAPTER 8

Candice watched as *The Flying Carpet* crash-landed, hanging parallel to the earth for an eternal moment before the forested ground seemed to lunge up to embrace it. Trees swarmed over it like ants over a carcass, shearing off its wings, tearing the tail section free to disappear into the smoke and detritus the crash kicked up. The fuselage plowed forward like a runaway train, smashing the trees in its path to splinters, buckling and contorting until it came to a precarious rest at the end of a long furrow in the woods. Smoke trailed from what remained of the hull, half-buried in the muck of the undergrowth—fire slowly spreading from the embers the crash had nearly snuffed out.

"Hit it again," Singh said.

Candice threw herself at him without conscious thought. "Singh, you motherfucker!" She didn't notice how Gore slipped behind her, neatly corralling her before she could reach his boss. She was barely aware that she'd stopped moving short of her target. "You made your point!"

Singh smiled at her. "Thank you. But I think it bears repeating. Hit them again."

"No!" Candice said even before he'd finished the order. "I'll do it! I'll do it! Whatever you want—I'll make the skull work."

Singh paused. "There, see?" He reached out to straighten Candice's collar. "Was that so hard? Change your mind again and… Well, if you thought that was hard to watch, I'll have Gore show you parts of yourself you'd normally need a vivisection to see."

The PA chimed before Candice could begin to think of how to respond to that. The pilot announced, "Everyone, please take your seats and buckle up. We're beginning our landing approach now."

Singh was all smiles. "And they say you can't get any business done on a flight."

Someone was laughing at Nevada. She didn't blame them. If you looked at it the right way, plane crashes were just the world's longest pratfalls.

She forced her eyes open. Above her, the color was draining from the evening sky. She could hear the cries of animals readying themselves for the night—the clicking calls of barking geckos, like a game of marbles played in fast-forward, and the chittering birdsong of plovers.

She straightened her head. It *pounded* vertiginously, like she was riding a roller coaster with every few degrees she moved. That nearly crowded out the aches and pains that competed for attention in her bruised body. If she was slow and careful, she could avoid outright nausea while staying in motion enough that the pain didn't settle on her—instead it stomped up and down on her like a mad gorilla. That made it the work of minutes to ascertain that she'd woken up with all the parts she'd had before going under.

All around her was grass as tall as her shoulder, glowing red-hot with the setting sun. Some kind of savanna, dotted with umbrella-like acacia trees as far as the eye could see. No people.

Look on the bright side: if there were people around, with your luck you'd land on the Wicked Witch of the East.

She could see all this because *The Flying Carpet* had come undone. The cockpit was still in one piece, but that piece didn't include the rest of the plane. The fuselage was scattered piecemeal in a trail of destruction behind them for what seemed like miles, one wing sticking up from the flattened landscape like a headstone. It looked, in short, like she felt.

Jacques. The thought hit her like a .45 slug, blanking out all the pain. Her hands flew to her seatbelt, ripping herself out of the buckles as she nearly broke her neck turning to see Jacques. He was half out of his seat, sprawled limp across the dashboard, all those dials and gauges he'd loved so much now soaking in his blood.

Finally loose, Nevada pulled him back fully into the pilot's seat, gritting her teeth against her own pain. It felt like hell, but she didn't have time for it. The bandage she'd made him was soaked through. She ripped off her other sleeve and pressed it into the wound as hard as she could.

Jacques groaned, coming out of his sleep and into pain. "*Mort sur le champ d'honneur*!"

Nevada felt bad for him. She'd feel worse if he were dead. "Jacques, you okay?"

"I think…" Jacques muttered, raising his head with obvious difficulty, "that must be the funniest joke you have ever told."

Blood from a gash on the side of his head ran from the corner of his left eye to into his hairline. Nevada glimpsed the white of bone inside it. She reached under her seat, finding a swath of maps that she wadded up to press to the cut. Maps were useless now. They weren't going anywhere in this bird. She felt a pang of emotion, separate and distinct from the pain flooding her body. *The Flying Carpet* had been one hell of a plane. Gotten them where they'd needed to go no matter how far. Never gave up on them even with spotty maintenance, rusted parts, and more holes in her than a cheese grater. She deserved better than being shot down, crashing in some godforsaken jungle. But Nevada supposed she wouldn't go out much better when it was her time.

"You'll be okay. You'll be fine. You've just gotta stop bleeding, that's what you gotta do—"

The laughter in the back of her mind kept going. Great, not only had her plane crashed, but she was having a stroke too.

"I think I have a concussion. I have had a concussion before. It felt a lot like this…"

"How bad a concussion can it be if you can remember another concussion?" Nevada put up her hand. "How many fingers am I holding up?"

Jacques squinted. "The same number of genders there are," he answered at length.

Nevada put her hand down. "Nice try."

She'd seen a lot of people die, but she'd never looked closely enough to see the life leave someone—the heft of the soul as it was borne away on whatever winds carried it. Jacques's eyes wandered. His expression slackened. Nevada slapped him hard enough to sting her own hand.

"Stay with me, Jacques. You can't die. It's not poetic enough. You have to die of consumption or liver failure or something. Not a plane crash." Nevada felt her throat tightening, barely letting words out. "C'mon. You're scaring me."

Jacques's eyes focused on a point that seemed slightly to the left of Nevada. "You've spent your whole life showing everyone that you're not afraid of anything, but Thea—didn't anyone ever tell you it's okay to be?"

Nevada fixed her hands to his cheeks like she could hold his life inside him, crush his soul down to fit into his body no matter how small it got. Suddenly he seemed very old and very small and very tired. "Hey, you know what? Next time we need money, let's just rob a fucking bank."

More laughing, behind her, echoing through the decapitated neck of the plane. Nevada turned.

"What is so *fucking* funny—"

She saw the spotted hyena, jaw yawning open, teeth thick and flat to crush bone. It was the first of six, a pack, prowling into the wreckage. Their screeching cackles echoed through the broken plane. Nevada placed herself between them and Jacques, her hands balled into fists.

"Laugh it up, fuzzball."

The lead hyena reared back onto his hind legs, his forepaws tight against his chest, then he launched himself at her in a riot of laughter. Nevada braced herself for the impact. It never came. A spear smoothly bisected the hyena's flight, jamming it against the wall of the plane. It slumped to the ground.

The other hyenas ran. They were still laughing.

Nevada didn't care who her savior was. She clapped Jacques's face a few more times, keeping him at least semiconscious, before she stepped out of the cockpit. "My friend, he's hurt, he needs help—"

Pygmies. Twenty of them. Not one reached five feet tall. They all wore loincloths or shorts, all held bows or spears. As Nevada stepped toward them, their weapons came up. Nevada froze in the middle of taut bowstrings and pointed spears.

One of them barked a command in a language Nevada wouldn't include on her resume. Another came forward, taking a length of rope off his shoulder. Nevada doubted she'd get any bonus points for deducing it was meant for her. Slowly, carefully, she held her arms out, wrists together, waiting to be tied.

"And they wonder why women go for tall men."

Candice was being driven to her death in what was certainly the most expensive car she'd ever ridden in.

It was an Italian car, sculpted like a razor to cut through the air. She sat in the second of its two seats, hands still bound in her lap. Gore drove, his hands confidently firm on the wheel. Ahead of them, a Land Rover filled with gunmen provided escort. Behind them was Singh's ride, a stretch limo, and behind that was another Land Rover. Despite the fact that they had to keep pace with the caravan, the sedan's engine roared with masculinity. The ride was whisper-smooth, but when Gore so much as toed the gas pedal, it sent a fleeting tremor through the frame of the car and into Candice's body, like a space shuttle taking off.

Perhaps she was overly sensitive. There wasn't much else to focus on in the featureless landscape and unadorned blacktop. Gore was as silent and watchful as a carrion bird as he coolly reclined in his seat, manipulating the steering wheel with evident pleasure. Candice supposed if she were in the driver's seat, she would enjoy driving however many millions of dollars had gone into this car too.

She shook her head. Here she was being driven from one prison to another, and she was admiring the ride. It made a sick sort of sense. If there was one thing she'd learned over the past few weeks, it was adaptability. The human body could become used to anything, even extremes. It grew immune to poison. It built up a tolerance to drugs. And now, unable to maintain a panic attack for every brush with death, her fear had given way to anger. Gore, Singh, and their whole conspiracy had hurt Easy, perhaps killed her. Candice couldn't even say why. As part of some labyrinthine plot, to ensure her cooperation for a task she didn't know how to do... Madness. She felt used up, but more than that, she was bitterly enraged. She could almost understand Nazir al-Jabbar and his hatred, but for Gore, it was only business. He felt *nothing*. She wanted to lash out at him. She wanted to draw blood before hers was inevitably taken.

"Are you going to say something? Or do you let your master do all the talking while you think of new ways to kill and torture people?"

Gore wasn't rattled. "No, I know most of them by now."

He gave her a sidelong glance that had Candice making herself as unthreatening as possible. Otherwise, his eyes consumed the road with barely an interest in her.

"I know what you're thinking," he said, now looking straight ahead. "How long until Nevada kills this asshole? Tick-tock, tick-tock. What's taking her so long?" He sneered. "I wouldn't get my hopes up."

"Keep telling yourself that."

Gore sighed. "You don't get it. You think you're the first? I've kept tabs on Nevada for a long time—had to make sure she wasn't skimming from the till. There was a redhead in Bangladesh, a blonde in Paris, a brunette in New Zealand. She does make friends easily. You're not even her first taste of brown sugar. That was in—I wanna say Brazil? So no. You're nothing special. Just her way of passing the time."

"You don't know anything about her or me," Candice told him. "What would you know about caring for someone else? It's obvious no one's ever cared about you."

"Maybe not. But I do have some good pictures of what Nevada 'caring for' someone looks like. I can show them to you later. You could tell me which of them she'd die for—since you're such an expert."

Candice was silent. Gore turned the steering wheel to follow a curve. The black sweat that gloved his fingers stayed on the wheel. Holding it with one hand, Gore took out a handkerchief and wiped away the stain.

"Every person's touch leaves oil and residue and fingerprints behind. The only difference is that you can see mine. Makes you think, doesn't it?" He lifted his eyes slightly. "We're here."

Ahead, the horizon was replaced by the sea, a pier jetting out a pathetically small distance into the endless expanse. Speedboats were docked there.

Candice thought about burials at sea.

Drums pounded like racing hearts. Torches flared, what little light they could shed eaten up by the darkness. Nevada could imagine that the vast untracked savanna, with its flourishes of isolated trees, might look epic in the day. In the night, the expanse of deep shadows and animal sound was imposing. If she fell off the trail she was following, she might fall forever into the inky, black abyss that surrounded her on all sides.

She'd been walking for what felt like hours, her hands bound, the Pygmies watching her closely. She might've tried something, only Jacques was bringing up the rear in a litter. The Pygmies had bandaged him, but he'd long since stopped speaking or moving. Occasionally Nevada would look back to reassure herself that his chest was still faintly in motion, but those pauses unfailingly earned her a prod from her captors. She did it anyway. Whatever happened to Jacques, she'd share in it. If he died on the road, she'd send battalions to join him.

What was worse, she'd noticed that she could only see out of one eye. It was impossible to examine herself closely on the trail, but when she touched her right eye, most of what she felt seemed to be dried blood. Not that she had a strong urge to take in the sights.

The pounding of the drums intensified, welcoming the war party or hunters or whoever they were home. In the swell, Nevada almost missed the sloshing of a river, right up until they were crossing over it on a creaking bridge. Reed and straw huts sprung up like mushrooms around Nevada as she was led into the center of the village on the bank of the river. The huts lit up—the smell of kerosene lanterns, the hum of buzzing electricity—and faces stared out at her, gawking, judging. Maybe deciding what side they should order. Nevada didn't exactly have a read on the situation. The Pygmies in front of her halted, she halted in turn, and the Pygmies behind her didn't prod her anymore. She guessed this was their stop.

"That's good drumming, but I have to be honest—girls only go for lead guitar," she said to unhearing, uncaring faces. "Does anyone here speak English? How about a doctor? Can we do that? My friend is hurt. He needs medical attention or he's going to die."

Silence. Motionlessness. Nevada could've ripped someone's head off, but she was tired from the march and still aching from the crash. She could only imagine the bruises she would have in the morning. If she made it that long.

"How about sign language?" Nevada asked sardonically. "Let's try that."

She brought her bound hands up to her mouth, biting into the rope and playing her fingers at the knot until it was loose, then looser, then off. The village exploded in uproar, armed Pygmies crowding in on her with spears held so close to her that if she breathed hard, she'd break the skin. Nevada set her teeth.

"*My friend needs help*. And if things don't start getting *Chicago Hope* up in here, I am going to play Whack-A-Mole with your entire society." A spearhead came into her field of vision, brushing her eyelashes. "And get that thing out of my face if you want *any* say in where it's going to be a minute from now."

Someone spoke—a few foreign words and the spearhead came away from her face. The crowd parted. Their Grand Poobah wore a headdress that added a foot to his height. He was still six inches shorter than most of the others. But maybe here that meant he was closer to nature, literally.

Clearing his throat, he spoke to her in English that was passable the same way the water in Flint was drinkable. "The great god asks your presence. You must come. He want you. Fat. Much food."

Nevada blinked. "Wow. Body-shaming? From Mini-Me? Same to you, buddy."

The spears in front of her cleared out while the spears behind her pressed in. Almost unthinkingly she walked forward, nestled in the middle of a ring of spears that only allowed her a few feet of free motion, and only in the direction they wanted her to go. They led her to a large hut, built on stilts to tower over the others the same way a food truck would tower over a lemonade stand. Nevada rolled her eyes. She'd planned to take down a billion-dollar oil tycoon, and now she was having trouble with Minions. This seemed like a bad sign.

The chieftain called up to the hut in his own tongue. There was no response. He called again, louder.

"If it helps," Nevada said, "you might want to tell him that I'm not kosher. Just throwing that out there."

Lights flared in the house, razoring out through the doorway and windows in a sickly and flickering yellow. Nevada heard the floorboards creak like a great weight had been put on them. Then footsteps. One a normal footfall, then a heavy thud. Discordant. Step, *thud*, step, *thud*. Until Nevada could see a silhouette emerge into her view of the interior—big, *hulking* big, limping closer and closer to the doorway. Step, *thud.* Until finally he reached the passage, stooped to pass through it, and came up to his full height outside. Six foot five if he was an inch, and two-fifty pounds easily. Not counting the metal prosthetic where the left leg had once been.

"Ah shit," Nevada said. "Not you."

CHAPTER 9

Candice watched Gore the same way she might watch a snake that had crawled into her tent. As the speedboat carried them both from the harbor, he lowered his hand into the water rushing by. It scoured his fingers of the black oil that tainted them. When his hand came back up, it was dripping clean.

Candice turned to look at their destination. She'd thought the ship was simply far away, but at their speed, it grew exponentially, dwarfing her expectations. It was an oil tanker, the name *Liparus* written on the side in big, blocky Cyrillic. Rusted and encrusted with barnacles, it looked halfway to being a shipwreck, which only added to its fearsome Soviet aura. It was simply enormous—a skyscraper turned on its side. A hulking juggernaut, its brute symmetry giving it an air of inevitability. Like some monstrous headstone over the world, it made her think endlessly of death. Candice felt a hateful certainty that she wouldn't leave the ship alive.

Gore dipped his other hand into the water. Candice heard the ripple of it washing his fingers clean. She closed her eyes and tried to free herself from the hold that the tension had on her. The cool spray of seawater against her body, the feeling of traveling over the waves, the smell of salt in the air—it wasn't unpleasant. Under other circumstances, she might've greatly enjoyed it. And if Nevada were there, even if she were tied up next to Candice… Nevada had a way of turning any difficulty, any misadventure, into something funny. Candice hadn't realized how much she would miss that when she was alone.

She opened her eyes, looking off to the side, scanning the horizon for the curvature of the Earth. As if somehow that would make it more likely for Nevada to come screaming out of nowhere with a half-baked plan and more firepower than seemed strictly necessary. It was hard to believe she'd known Nevada for such a short time; so briefly that certain details hadn't had a fair chance to imprint themselves in her memory. She couldn't remember the exact shade of Nevada's hair or if her eyes were blue or green. It made Candice feel infinitely careless, like she had squandered something precious.

Candice ducked her head. The truth was, she missed Nevada. Not for the hope that Nevada could rescue her or the protection that Nevada could offer her, but simply because she felt incomplete without her.

They passed under the shadow of the *Liparus*, its thousand and a half feet of length keeping the speedboat in darkness for long minutes.

Somewhere in high school, Butch had left behind the gawky twerp Nevada had grown up with and become so himself that he might as well have been a universal constant. Whatever the year, whatever the place, his wide, kind face was always the same: a mop of girl-long hair, a rakish blond beard, eyes as bright and happy as a puppy's. Then the broad shoulders and almost rudely excessive height of a linebacker, like a Viking with a golden retriever as his Power Coin. A man with no discernible malice in his rangy body, even as the force in its muscles was undeniable.

He looked exactly like the kind of guy who would own a pair of nunchucks. A Hawaiian shirt, aloha silkies, and a flip-flop on his one remaining foot, the other leg thudding into the ground with pure metal.

Butch winced as he looked her over. "God, you look worse than Katy Perry as a blonde."

"You're the one going full-on flip-flop. One leg and you've gotta put a flip-flop on it," Nevada said.

"Look around," Butch said. "Everyone's wearing sandals. You're the weirdo. You're wearing shoes."

"Just tell me you have a doctor," Nevada said, nodding to Jacques.

Butch went to examine him, whistling to get the Pygmies' attention and then calling out a few native words. "Oh man," he grimaced at Jacques's state, "SpongeBob is this close to having to get a new narrator..."

"*Doctor*," Nevada insisted.

"He's coming," Butch said, aggravated. And then there was motion in the crowd, the villagers getting out of the way to let one man by with a first-aid kit. "Good guy, went to Johns Hopkins, got a degree, then came back here to serve his community. You'd think that'd be super interesting, but it's actually a pretty lame story."

The doctor wore hiking shoes instead of the usual sandals, but he had on a goatskin kaross for a top and something like a coonskin cap on his head, only made out of what Nevada thought was a genet. He also wore jean shorts; Nevada couldn't help but wonder if that was less fashionable than the goatskin.

Nevada tuned Butch out, all her focus on the alleged doctor as he checked Jacques over. He seemed to know what he was doing: taking Jacques's pulse, then listening to his breathing. Finally, he went to Butch, speaking with him in hushed tones. Nevada found herself pressing in on them to overhear. Butch noticed her intruding on the conversation and gave the doctor a quick look, motioning to Nevada.

The doctor turned to her and spoke in English. "He'll need surgery to set a few bones and remove the bullet, but it missed the vital organs. His breathing's strong and his heartbeat's steady. He'll be fine."

Nevada sighed in relief and was surprised to feel how much the motion taxed her. On the trail, there'd been a kind of numbness holding her bruises off, but now every bit of having been battered and bashed was setting into her flesh. She felt like she'd been through a meat grinder.

"What about you?" Butch put in, reaching out his hand to brush the hair out of Nevada's face and away from her injured eye. "Where'd you get the hole in your face, learning to eat with a fork?"

Nevada batted his hand away but let the doctor examine her. He shined a penlight into her damaged eye, and Nevada had a vague impression of its light, but nothing as absolute as she would've thought having a light glaring into her eyeball would get.

"Definite damage, but it looks intact. We'll need to bandage it. I don't want that exposed."

"I'll handle that," Butch said. "You take care of Gramps."

He stooped to get supplies out of the first aid kit and took Nevada aside, sitting her down on a rock as he looked her over. Nevada kept her eye on Jacques, watching as the doctor and some assistants picked his litter up and carried him, presumably to whatever passed for an operating theater here. Butch covered her injured eye with a pad.

"Hold that, would you?" Nevada did, and Butch taped it in place. "You get a Christmas gift for Mom yet?"

"I have one in my Amazon cart. I'm just waiting until I need to buy something else so I can get the free shipping."

Butch looped linen wrapping around her injured eye and its shield to hold it in place. "I just realized I don't have *Goodfellas* on Blu-Ray. You could get that for me, and I'll pay you back."

"Of course it's a mob movie," Nevada muttered.

She tried to force herself to relax. With the emergency over, the suspense the Pygmies had been in was crumbling. Now they moved about with whatever chores could occupy their last hours of wakefulness. Women stooped from place to place with bundles balanced on their heads; men carved knickknacks that Nevada supposed would be hawked at some nearby tourist trap.

Jacques had disappeared into a shanty of corrugated tin. His blood was trampled into the ground; his trauma faded into the scenery. It made Nevada want to scream somehow.

"So what's with the Oompa-Loompas?" she asked.

Butch grimaced as he tied the bandage off. "Excuse me, they prefer to be called the Lollipop Guild, thanks. Anyway, it's a long story. I'll explain on the way back to *mi casa es su casa*. We haven't got a lot of time."

Nevada let his Spanish go unmolested. "Why? What's the rush?"

"I have a pizza in the oven."

"Does it have pineapple on it?"

"No."

"Okay then, what are we waiting for?" she said, shooting to her feet. She couldn't be tired without being numb, and she couldn't be numb when she hurt this bad.

Candice's blood pounded a dirge against her temples as the speedboat sloshed to a stop. They were beside the impossible bulk of the tanker, the prow of their own boat gently tapping its enormous hull. A gantry grew up the side of the hull like a varicose vein, bright orange with non-corroding metal. As she and Gore waited, a freight elevator descended the scaffolding. The entire thing was an open-air elevator shaft.

The elevator and its occupant, a crew member in a red jumpsuit, shuffled to a stop. He opened the cage door and, with little more than a nod, traded places with Gore. Candice thought of shoving them into the water and taking the boat, but there was no chance she'd figure out the controls before Gore put a bullet in her. She climbed into the elevator, Gore secured the door, and the crew member turned the speedboat to shore as the elevator ascended.

Candice watched the ocean's surface march away from her until she couldn't take it anymore, her stomach rebelling from the height. She told herself that it was no different from being in any elevator, especially the glass kind that actually let her see the building she was climbing. But the grated floor and accordion gate opened the elevator car to the elements, showing her in the starkest, simplest terms imaginable how she was going up two hundred feet in the air. The wind whistled, buffeting her, a chilling caress on her spine. When the ride ended, she was as high as the Leaning Tower of Pisa. At this height, if she jumped, she'd hit the water so fast that it might as well be concrete.

Gore drew open the gate and brought her out onto the deck. The *Liparus* was as wide as an apartment block, while its length sprawled out to either side for what seemed like miles, as long as two of the pyramids at Giza laid next to each other. And every inch of it manmade metal, clonking underfoot with each step she took. Candice had known Singh had resources, but this… It was like inevitability made tangible.

There was a welcome party waiting for them. Four guards, armed, in red jumpsuits, and one academic-looking type. A preening tall man, balding but with an uncomfortably lush moustache, his sparse physique sagging at the middle like a poorly built bridge. He wore a parka over a lab coat over a twill shirt and slacks. He looked so out of place that Candice wondered if he was a prisoner too, but no. No one in fear for his life could stand so calmly, so devoid of worry, as untouched by the dangers of the world as a cow in its pasture.

Urged on by Gore, Candice walked toward them. The guards clocked her, shifted to subtly ready their weapons for her. *Not yet, lads*, Candice wanted to tell them. *I'm still useful for now.*

Away from the shifting balance of the sea, everything seemed preordained, fated. Each footstep brought up an echoing clang. Each breath overwhelmed her nostrils with the harshly noxious smell of oil, drowning out the briny tang of the ocean.

"Dr. Cushing!" The man waved. He spoke good English with a slight Flemish accent. "It's so good to meet you at last! I have been briefed on your qualifications. If we're going to have a fresh set of eyes on our little problem, I'm glad they're so expert." He offered his hand. "Alfred Jansen."

"Nice to meet you," Candice said, nodding pleasantly at him. "I've been kidnapped."

Jansen looked for a moment like he'd swallowed something without chewing enough. "Ah, well, one is often asked to press on despite unfortunate circumstances."

"What're yours?" Candice asked him.

He demurred, and Gore spoke instead. "Let's move along. No need to get held up."

To Candice's surprise, he didn't head to the stern of the boat. She knew from an otherwise long-forgotten magazine article that the white tower there was the bridge, engine room, and crew quarters, with a three-story engine to push the giant oil tanks that took up the majority of the ship's double hull.

Instead, Gore walked to what looked like a flat cellar door on the deck, one more feature on the *Liparus*'s four blood-red football fields of space, broken up by pipes and vents and other miscellany Candice couldn't guess at. White safety railings marked a path through what otherwise could have been a labyrinth of thorns surrounding Sleeping Beauty's castle.

Gore threw open the horizontal doors. A few steps led down to a grated footplate, waist-deep under the doors. Two of the guards and Jansen went first. Candice followed once it became clear that the other two guards were waiting for her. They came in after her; Gore hit the push button on a pendant control station. After a beep, the grate lowered itself through the ship's hull. Another elevator—this one inside the *Liparus*.

The elevator cleared the hull, descending into what had to be the cargo hold. Candice felt like she'd been submerged in quicksilver. The interior of the tanker was all but empty, a vast space dominated by nothingness, reminding her of a blimp hangar. Or a massive vault. Or a tomb. The walls, ceiling, and floor were chrome, uninterrupted from the top of the ship to the bottom, going for a quarter mile from the bow to the stern. The only light came from work lamps set up along either wall, but the light they shone was reflected a thousand times over into a harsh glare that came from all directions. Here and there, she could see more of Singh's jump-suited minions milling about, attending to small tasks she was too far away to see in any detail. They seemed to line up, though, their bodies forming a sporadic chain from the front of the space to the back.

"Quite impressive, isn't it?" Jansen asked ingratiatingly. "I realize the conditions—I mean, for you personally—they leave something to be desired. But in time, I think you'll see you're truly fortunate to be a part of a real scientific breakthrough!"

Candice turned to him. "Or you could call the police."

Jansen laughed uncomfortably. Gore just stared at them both.

"Oh no, no," Jansen continued. "You really just have to—well, try to see it's best to make the most out of things, so to speak. Just think of all the people who'd love to trade places with you! It's not so bad here—we have an exercise room, an entertainment center, the kitchen can make vegetarian meals..."

"Wasting your time, Doc," Gore said, looking past them.

Candice followed his gaze. He was watching the workmen, and by straining her eyes, Candice could see they were toiling over a set of tracks laid across the floor. Like a mine-cart track only bigger.

Candice couldn't begin to speculate on what tracks like these were for. Distracted and anxious, she felt like picking at the scab that was Jansen some more, but what was the point? He wasn't going to jeopardize whatever Singh had offered him, especially not at this late stage.

He just had to put up with a few gray areas, a little bending of the rules, to get what he wanted—whatever the crystal skulls had to give his particular project. And the closer he got, the more he was willing to bend. Candice could understand that all too well. She'd put her own life in jeopardy going with Nevada to find the skull in the first place. But that was her own life. Not other people's.

Despite everything, she, too, felt an excitement to know what the skulls actually *were*. What they could do, and what that might possibly mean to mankind. Thoughts like this were better than dwelling on how her stomach lurched in a mixture of vertigo and seasickness. As inevitable as the rattling slog of the elevator she was on.

They trudged to a stop. Two guards remained in the elevator while the other two, along with Candice, Gore, and Jansen, left through the opening in the railing. The others immediately circled around and went the other way, stepping past the elevator. Candice turned around, as reluctant to leave the comparative safety of the elevator as she was eager to get all the suspense over with.

A dozen yards to the rear was an isolation chamber; a cube of reinforced glass ten feet on all sides, tented in plastic for an additional layer of secure insulation, the draping folds giving it a vaguely pyramidal outline. The only entrance or exit was an airlock jutting out of one wall like a maw and throat, a short corridor pointing at Candice, beginning and ending with sliding glass doors. Both inner and outer doors were closed.

Another party was gathered around the chamber. Scientists or technicians in lab coats, with standing workstations circling the chamber. In the middle of all the gleaming, sci-fi chrome, the bustle of weird activity struck Candice as some sort of pagan altar, an exhibition on primordial life in the middle of an ultramodern museum.

She approached it, feeling foolish for having missed the sight just because it was in her blind spot. And even that blushing embarrassment curdled bitterly. What if she'd missed a possibility to escape? Some observation that could save her life?

No time for recriminations either. She'd find whatever chink in the armor there was. Whatever Singh's resources, he was a madman, an imbecile. Way too much of an idiot to idiot-proof his scheme.

You have to out-idiot the idiots and their idiot-proofing. The thought struck Candice as so much something Nevada would say that a pang of need came over her. She couldn't remember ever having held Nevada, having been embraced by her. She needed the feeling of her back.

A Barcalounger sat in front of the isolation chamber, as out of place among the sprawl of metal as the chilly glass and mummifying plastic. Although in an environment this surreal, Candice didn't know what would be in place. Singh sat in the chair, the mad prophet of whatever gnostic cult was laboring before him. Candice came to a stop beside his chair. For a moment, she simply took in the scale of the operation: the retrofitted tanker, the laboratory set up within its hold, the army of security—Nevada had thought this was some hobby, but it wasn't. It was an obsession. Endless resources brought to bear.

This close, she could see the twelve crystal skulls inside the chamber. Three were lined up against each wall on top of pedestals. Wires ran down from each one's cradle and tangled under the floor. Candice could only imagine the sensors trained on them. And still they were a mystery.

The quartz skulls swirled chaotically with whorls of color and light, shaped impossibly into a series of death heads. Not human, but not deformed either. Some strange symmetry held them, blots of hallucinogenic color within the antiseptic white that surrounded them and the featureless metal that surrounded that. In this insane landscape, they almost seemed rational.

"Beautiful, aren't they?" Singh asked. He didn't look at her. His eyes drank in the skulls like he never wanted to look at anything else. "I like to be alone with them sometimes. Like they might whisper something to me. I guess they kinda did. They just relayed it to you first."

Candice felt like she was babysitting some bratty child who demanded ice cream for breakfast. "I don't know how they work. I don't know what I did or didn't do. Nothing's going to happen if I go in there."

Singh looked at her, his eyes sunken in their sockets—Candice wondered when he'd last slept. "Then why are you so nervous?" he said.

Candice said nothing.

"Put her in. I've waited for this long enough."

"Wait," Candice said sharply, but Gore collared her, one arm bent behind her back, a hand on her shoulder to force her forward to the airlock leading into the chamber. Its first door slid open with a hiss of equalizing glasses.

Candice could see she wouldn't be able to make any difference fighting. At most, they'd gang up on her, pick her up bodily and throw her into the airlock. She went along and Gore applied a little less force, letting go of her as she came to the cusp of the airlock so she could go in under her own power. If it was meant to be some sort of grace note, Candice didn't want it. She turned around and gave him the V.

The outer door of the airlock shut.

Butch's driver was four feet tall, adult features in a child's frame, and the boundless energy that went with the latter. He hummed and weaved in place as he drove—wooden blocks tied to his feet to let him reach the pedals.

The night was pitch black, no streetlights or road reflectors to relieve it, not even the moon or stars. The only light came from the headlights of the Volkswagen Type 181 they rode in, setting the unpaved road on fire in front of them. The weak taillights snuffed the fire out just as quickly.

The speedometer was at sixty, not that there seemed to be any motion, with the darkness exactly the same in all directions. Even the road didn't seem to change; always more winding, twisting convolutions of dirt. The wild driving almost managed to outpace Nevada's need to keep moving, or maybe the crash had spoiled her taste for it a little. Maybe it was the four Vicodin tablets Butch had given her. For some reason, she was sure she could *feel* the bruises developing where her seatbelt had tried to guillotine her.

They turned a corner, maybe. Now there was light on the horizon. A weird glow boiled off smoke, as if the stars and the clouds had crashed to earth, the harvest moon breaking open like the yolk of an egg.

Nevada kneaded her sinuses. God, she was tired. Maybe her eyes were closed and she was seeing the surges of color that came from squeezing eyelids together. Then the color was gone, crushed down into a smudged line as if the sun were coming up prematurely.

"Okay, am I imagining that?" Nevada asked, aggravated. "Because my imagination has done a lot better. It must be slacking off."

Butch was nearly invisible in the spillage from the headlights, but Nevada could just about see him cup a hand above his eyes, even though it was night. *Idiot.*

"No, that would be a wildfire. Couple weeks off, though."

"Wildfire?"

"Yeah. Check it out!" Butch pointed, and the glow burst back into being as if on cue. It reminded Nevada of pressing a Duracell battery into steel wool and watching it burn out, only the steel wool was a good chunk of her world at the moment. "The fire's dune-walking. It goes into these valleys and there's less grass for it to burn, but then it comes up the other side—whoosh!"

"Whoosh," Nevada repeated.

"Yeah. Bushmen, y'know? They can track their prey better without all the grass in the way. And it makes it easier to find bauhinia nuts, which I personally don't like the taste of, but it's like a McRib sandwich to them."

Nevada lay back against her seat and shut her eyes. The world was on fire. Made sense. "Butch?"

"Yeah, Sis?"

"Why do you have Pygmies now?"

"It's a little complicated." Nevada heard the backseat heave as he settled down next to her. "You know in *Black Panther*, how Wakanda is all advanced and peaceful and everyone gets along?"

"Yeah, I only saw it in *Infinity War*, but I got the gist."

"Well, the Bandar are from one of those African countries that isn't like that. Lots of war and famine, plague, glutens, all kinds of shit. They came here and settled on this parcel of land. The government said they could stay, so all of a sudden this estate is kinda a white elephant. Because it's covered in Pygmies. Just lousy with 'em."

"Okay. And you own the land?"

Butch nodded so enthusiastically that Nevada cracked an eyelid just to see it. "Uh-huh! Got it at a steal. The guy who owns it can't develop it because of all the Pygmies. So we're playing poker, right, and he is two hundred thousand dollars in the hole…"

Both her eyes popped open. "You won two hundred thousand dollars playing poker?"

"It was a long game," Butch demurred. "He's losing another hand when he tells me he doesn't have two hundred thousand dollars, but he does have this land."

"Useless land," Nevada clarified. "Full of Bandar Pygmies?"

"Yes," Butch agreed readily. "But that's not the good part. See, the Bandar believe—well, I don't know quite what they believe, but they think that God owns the land they live on, so since I own the land… I'm God."

Nevada closed her eyes again. "Butch, let me ask you something. Seeing as you're these people's god, have you done anything to improve their standard of living?"

"Oh yeah, I let them steal cable from me all the time. And I told them to quit doing clitoridectomies." Butch tugged at his collar. "Always saw that as kind of a fifty-fifty thing. Like, good news is, we found it. Bad news…"

"So a bunch of short people think you're God," Nevada interrupted. "What does that accomplish?"

"I don't know yet," Butch admitted. "But there's got to be some money in it. Look at Tom Cruise!"

Nevada rested her head against the window glass. The shudders of the road in motion lulled her as close to sleep as she could get with the tension she carried keeping her awake. As they came to a stop to let a herd of rhinos pass, she thought she saw Butch snarl a grin and say, "You're really not going to say anything, are you?" But it wasn't like she could double-check. Not with only one eye. She sighed. Snide remarks she could deal with. All-out drama she didn't have time for. Hopefully he would save the emotion until he got drunk, like a normal person.

Butch's estate appeared out of the night like a puzzle putting itself together. First the car settled down onto paved road. After the potholes and ruts of the dirt trail, it was like being in the palm of God's hand. The grass became a finely manicured lawn. Then they swung by a gate. The road changed again, from cobblestone to pavement, and the mansion swam into the view of the jeep's headlights.

Dutch Colonial. Candice would love that. The main house was the size of a barn, huddling under a gable roof, with two wings projecting out on stilts—balconies, Nevada supposed. The garage was an open-air affair under the one to the left.

"Put on your shoes, hon. We're at Grandma's," Butch said.

Inside, it was a gentleman's club—the kind of place where the dress code called for a monocle. Huge chandeliers hung overhead, and gilded railings swung along stairways and catwalks. Stuffed hunting trophies were displayed like statues, faded oil portraits on the walls like funhouse mirrors for the house's intended occupants. Personally, Nevada only had first cousins and closer in her family photos, but she could see how it'd be different for the landed class. Something to reassure the owner that his weak chin went back seven generations.

The intensity of her brother's bachelorhood had overwhelmed the place. It was decorated in Early Pizza Box period, with some daring touches of Crumpled Beer Can. Against one wall was a pile of DVD cases. Nevada clucked her tongue.

"What?" Butch asked, making his way to the kitchen. *Thud, thud, thud...*

"You're just going to pile all your shit against the wall?"

"I stack it against the wall," Butch said from the other room.

"You can't buy a shelf? Maybe sell one of the stuffed tigers to finance it?"

"Hey, Hobbes really ties the room together. And what's wrong with saving money?"

"Nothing," Nevada said. "This would be a superb collection if you were a Cro-Magnon. If there were a DVD collection at Lascaux, it would look like this. Maybe if crows collected DVDs..."

Butch came out of the kitchen, carrying a tray of pizza in one hand and an icepack in the other. Elsewhere in the front room—which was so massive that Nevada thought it could do with being mapped—there was an assortment of chairs and sofas huddled around a coffee table. Butch set the pizza down on top of it, spilling a few battered paperbacks to the ground, and seated himself.

Nevada ducked her head as he took off his prosthetic and liner. Just above the amputation site, he had a tattoo of a stencil line, a little pair of scissors at the apex of his thigh. Weird how the two of them had the same sense of humor, and yet sometimes she didn't find him funny at all.

Butch pressed the icepack to his stump. "C'mon. Eat. I don't know how many pizzas the body needs to get over being in a plane crash, but it's definitely got to be at least two slices."

Nevada went over to the oasis of furniture in a wasteland of unvacuumed carpet. "No pepperoni?"

Butch shook his head. "I gave up meat for Lent."

"You're Catholic now? When did that happen?"

Whatever Butch's answer was, it was muffled by the bite of pizza he took. Nevada picked up her own slice. Overlooking the coffee table was a corkboard stuffed to overflowing with maps, drawings, runic translations, and pictures of Norse artifacts. Colored string and pushpins formed some sort of pattern—mostly it just looked like one of those cars with a billion bumper stickers on it. All Butch needed was Calvin peeing somewhere...

"Still trying to find Thor's hammer or whatever? Would you even be able to lift it? I mean, how many abs do you have, two?"

"Hey, I don't make fun of your stupid fantasies. Atlantis. Camelot. A female president…" Butch circled his hand in the air as if running through them all. "Could you go get some beer? I'd go, but my leg's off."

"Sure. I'll go. I've only been through a crash landing today."

"Emphasis on *landing*," Butch called after her.

The kitchen was spotless, right out of HGTV, but Nevada didn't credit Butch any self-discipline for that. There were three packages on the island: paper plates, paper bowls, and red Solo cups. And there was a drying rack by the sink for metal utensils. If Butch even knew how to turn a dishwasher on, there was no sign of one.

Nevada went to the fridge. "Hey, Butch, you ever think about remodeling this place? Maybe going in for a package of straws? You could go buck-wild and get the crazy kind."

"I live a life of spartan simplicity," Butch yelled from the other room.

"If the Spartans had known about cheese graters, they would've had one."

She opened the refrigerator. It was wall-to-wall bachelor chow, but there were some fruits and vegetables too. She picked something called Chibuku Shake from the top shelf. It was in a blue and white paper package that made it look more like milk than anything else, but there was a warning on it about walking drunk on the road, so either it had alcohol in it or the milk in South Africa dispensed general life advice.

She took the carton and two Solo cups to Butch.

"What do you feel like doing about Jacques?" Butch asked her, taking the carton and shaking it up. Maybe it was a protein shake. A protein shake with alcohol in it. That actually didn't sound too bad right about now.

"What do you mean?"

Butch poured for both of them. "My flock—"

"Oh brother," Nevada interjected.

"Yes," Butch said simply. "They'll take him to the hospital; he'll wake up there—probably too much to hope for that he's going to be in a coma until you're finished with all the murder you need to get done."

"Divinity's given you very good manners, Butch." Nevada picked up her cup. "You want to send flowers or balloons?"

"I don't know. If I recall, when I woke up with a severe knee deficiency, you sent me a Get Well Soon card."

Nevada sat down across from him. "And if I recall, I was a little busy finding crystal skulls to nurse you back to health."

Butch slugged down his portion of Chibuku like it had pissed him off. "Yeah, you give your kid up for eight years, he gets a brain tumor, and suddenly you're mother of the year. Come on..."

Nevada squeezed her eyes shut. She didn't want to feel rattled, she didn't want to argue—she couldn't. Let Butch be pissed off. She could patch that up later. There wasn't any time now. "I came here for information."

Butch gestured his cup around so dismissively that the Chibuku nearly sloshed out of it. "Yeah, yeah, I put feelers out, made sure all the usual suspects knew that if they have anything on this Singh guy and they come to me, I'll be appreciative." He drank again, shuddering as it went down. "And now you're here. Because I have something you want."

"You knew the risks. You wanted to be there. 'He's your son, but he's my nephew,' remember?"

Butch set his cup down on the coffee table, tapping it a few times on the flat surface. Nevada remembered he used to tap his foot when he got aggravated. His left foot. "Yeah, that's true. I wanted to be there. Just like I would've been there if you'd kept the baby instead of giving it to Goodwill. Now you're so desperate to avoid admitting that you made a mistake that you'll do anything to make this adoption scheme work."

Nevada took a drink; this didn't seem like a sober conversation. The Chibuku tasted like it'd been brewed out of oatmeal. Sour oatmeal. "He'd still be sick if I'd homeschooled him, or whatever it is you wanted me to do."

Sounding off deep in his throat, Butch snatched up his liner and rolled it over his stump. His fingers jittered with angry energy. "Yeah, he'd be sick, but you'd still know him. It was an open adoption, Sis. You can go see him whenever you want. You can tell him what happened. But you can't live with seeing him, and you can't live with staying away, so you do this. Say it works. Say he lives another eighty years. Are you just going to go back to pretending he doesn't exist?"

Nevada sank back in her chair and killed the screaming match that wanted to get out of her, killed it as many times as it came back. He was angry about his leg. It had nothing to do with the kid. He just needed to crash into her a few times, and since he wasn't the type to hit a woman, this was how he did it.

"That's none of your business, Butch."

"He was my best friend, Thea. Best guy I ever knew. Only man I could ever see being good enough for my sister. You ever think about him, or do you just pretend that didn't happen either?"

Nevada killed the screaming one more time. "You didn't know him like I did."

"What, did he eat crackers in bed?" Butch demanded, pulling his prosthetic on next. It clicked onto the liner. "You run. That's what you do. No wonder you call yourself Easy—whenever it gets hard, you bail."

"And you couldn't keep up!" Nevada snapped. "You wanna be pissed off about that, go do it in a mirror. I never asked you to come along."

"You didn't have to; I thought that was the point. What was I supposed to do, let Jacques watch your back?"

"We managed."

"Up till now."

"Do you have any intel, or could this have waited until the family reunion?"

Butch stood, pulling his pantleg around the end of the prosthetic. "Yeah. Someone either in Singh's organization or who's been watching it for a while. She has files on all his off-the-books operations, which I assume this would fall under."

"Yeah, no, I don't think they send out press releases about this sort of thing," Nevada spat out, not that even she believed her bitterness was directed at Singh. Not that it could be directed at Butch either.

"So I've set up a meet for tomorrow. You can look through her files and then be on your merry way. Wouldn't want to slow you down."

Nevada let that lie. She already felt like she'd shot herself in the foot by getting into it with him.

Appropriate.

"What's the name of the contact?"

Butch snapped his fingers a few times, cuing himself to remember. "She has one of those name-names, y'know? Yeah, it's—" The phone rang. Butch growled like a dog having its bone taken away. "Telemarketers. Excuse me while I find out that my car warranty is about to expire."

Nevada looked up at the ceiling, listening as he walked a few steps away. His prosthetic thudded right through the carpet. Then he turned back to her, cupping his cell phone against his chest.

"Do you know a Candice Cushing?"

CHAPTER 10

Candice saw two things through the glass of the airlock to the isolation chamber. One was her own reflection, translucent, ghostly, like she'd already died. The second was Gore. He took his gun from his holster, letting his arm hang at his side as if to show how comfortable he was with the weight. Candice got the message. She stepped through the airlock's inner door. It slid shut behind her. She was alone with the skulls, outnumbered twelve to one.

An intercom crackled; she jumped.

"Go do that voodoo that you do so well," Singh told her as her heart raced slightly less.

Candice approached one of the skulls. She wondered, vaguely, if it was the one she had found in the desert. Her heart was thundering, lungs pumping, blood sizzling—she wasn't in a state to discern fine details. She supposed it didn't matter.

"Shazam," she tried.

The skull laid there. Inanimate matter. Modern art.

The intercom squealed like a pig in heat. "Try harder, Ms. Cushing."

Candice glared at him through the glass and the gently wavering plastic sheeting. "Oy, I don't know if you've been keeping track, but I have a *much* better track record when it comes to these things than you do. If you wanna try, be my guest, yeah?"

More screeching from the intercom. Of all the things for a billionaire to skimp out on, why an intercom? This time, Jansen spoke. "Ms. Cushing, there are some theories we'd like to run by you. The first item: are you currently or have you been recently menstruating?"

"*Shut him up*," Candice hissed to Gore. "Hell with it."

She picked the skull up. The intercom sounded like it was having a taser shoved in it, but she ignored that, fixing all of her attention on the crystal face staring back at her.

"Listen. I don't know what you are. I don't know how this works. Maybe you're a bomb, maybe you're a genie—I don't care. If you're going to do something, do something. If it's bad—do it to them too. But enough with the paperweight act, you bloody—*numbskull*!"

Movement. Candice froze. She'd definitely seen something move, somewhere deep in the skull, like a fly wiggling its leg despite being trapped in amber. She looked closer. Iridescent color shimmered towards her, mesmerizing her. The skull had the coloring of an oil slick, a pearl, a snake, growing brighter and brighter, overwhelming. She blinked, but it did nothing to reduce the press of colors from inside the skull. There was no inside the skull. The colors were all around her in nebulas of amorphous radiance, erasing the outside world that would be there if she looked away.

She couldn't look away.

She was traveling through a galaxy inside the skull, her thoughts grasping and clutching into the storm of colors, something grasping and clutching back at her. She remembered reading somewhere that everyone's mind had a whole world in it—worlds within worlds. She felt like she was looking into someone else's world. Her eyes hurt. She had to turn her head to look away because her eyes couldn't move, but the skulls were on all sides of her, each of them glowing, filling the chamber with whirls of light, color so luminous it was painted on every surface, on her, on the insides of her eyelids when she blinked. The skulls met her gaze wherever she looked. She was trapped inside a geode, locked in a room full of mirrors and finding out where the reflection went when the mirrors reflected each other into infinity. There was always another reflection, a room within the room, and something at the center of it all, something it was all hiding … protecting? Guarding? *Caging*?

Then the glow was dying down. Candice felt the connection break, and it was like coming to after nearly nodding off—full wakefulness burying the haze of dreams. The skulls were all—at the same time, in the same way—darkening, growing cold and dull until they were once more hunks of crystal. Fireplaces with the flames snuffed out.

She set the skull back down, and the sounds of the outside world came crashing in, no intercom necessary.

"Bring them back!" Singh was shouting. He was standing right outside the chamber. "Make them do that again!"

Jansen was off in his own little world, muttering to himself.

Gore seemed on edge, his eyes wide like some hunted animal, nervously stroking the butt of his gun with his thumb. Candice made eye contact with him. Waited for him to register her. Let him know that he was afraid when she wasn't.

The intercom made stuck pig sounds. "Pick it up again!" Singh demanded. "I want them lighting up again!"

Jansen's voice came along for the ride, still coming from his own world. "The instruments didn't register any energy output, only tachyon particles—an outpouring of tachyons…"

Candice picked up the skull, but she knew nothing would happen. Nothing did. "It's done. It's finished."

"Not very many tachyons," Jansen continued, "but nothing else—not anything—everything is slightly radioactive, but I can't read anything from the skulls, nothing."

"Jansen!" Singh yelled, taking the bridge out from underneath his train of thought. "Do what I'm paying you for!"

"What's that?" Jansen asked haplessly.

"I don't know! Something!"

Jansen keyed the intercom. This time, it only made a tone before letting his voice through. "Try picking up another one of the skulls."

For some people, there was only so much higher education could do. Candice picked up another skull. It was as cold and lifeless as the first one, as all the rest were. "Show's over. Tip your waitress."

Singh wheeled on Jansen. "How long have you been working on this project?"

"This project? Well, I do believe I started on a leap year, so—"

"What's ten more seconds?" Singh asked. "Get them to work now."

Candice backed away, closing her eyes, covering her ears, but she could still hear Jansen's quavering voice. Her nerves were drawn so taut, she could hear the waves slapping against the hull.

"Ten—ten seconds? Well, I—this all bears further testing. I can't—I mean—I can't pull an answer—there's no answer I can give you in ten—you can do what you like, but I can't just *know more* about—you're just going to have to kill me."

"No, I won't," Singh said. "I have him."

Candice heard Gore's pistol go off. She'd known it was coming. It still made her jump.

She opened her eyes. Jansen was on the floor. His face was turned away from her; that was good. She didn't want to see how much was left of it.

Candice pictured a magician performing sleight of hand. *You see what he wants you to see. Worlds within worlds within everyone.* Her mind was grasping for something, anything, as if she'd fallen and she needed something to grab onto before she could get up.

Singh turned to her. "You're up. Gore, take her to her quarters. If the late Dr. Jansen deserved ten seconds, surely the lovely Candice Cushing can have until she's had some food."

Candice wasn't hungry. "I know how to make them work."

Singh stopped short. He wasn't moving, but he stopped breathing, blinking, probably even thinking. He just seemed to stare rapturously at her. "What?"

"The skulls. You want them glowing again? I know how."

Singh laughed shrilly and clapped Gore on the arm. "You hear that, Gore? The future is female. I've always believed that. Candice—sweet, sweet Candice—whenever you're ready."

Candice nodded. "I want to talk to Easy Nevada."

Now Singh blinked. "What?"

"Easy Nevada. I'd like to talk to her." She leaned against the side of the isolation chamber. "You don't mind if I make a long-distance call, do you?"

Singh brought his hands to his hair as if he were about to tear it out but instead dragged his palms down his face, steepling them under his chin. "I could kill you. Right now. I wouldn't even have to ask. I'd just point at you, and Gore, he'd—" Singh howled with sudden laughter. "You saw what happened to Jansen, yes?" Singh pointed at the body. "*That*… but *you*!" he concluded, pointing at Candice.

She nodded in consideration. "If you do that, you'll never get them to work."

"We'll figure them out!" Singh roared.

Candice sat down on the floor, crossing her legs under her. "I'll wait."

Singh looked at Gore. "What are you standing there for? Call Nevada or tweet her or *something*! And get that body out of here. I hear dead people shit themselves when they die and that is just—unhygienic."

Butch jerked his hand back after Nevada snatched the phone from him. "Watch it! I'm already down five toes. I can't lose a finger too."

"I know how hard counting is for you." Nevada pressed the phone to her ear. "Hello?" She brought the phone away to look at it. It was a FaceTime call. She pressed the little camera icon, and Candice's face filled the screen.

She'd heard the expression "a weight lifted off your shoulders," but this was more like waking up from a nightmare. She simply stared at Candice's full lips, her sweetly curved cheeks, her eyes like portions of the night sky. She wanted to thank Candice, bless her really, for being alive. She wanted to memorize her face for the eternity that each minute without her would be. She wanted to tell her how she felt but knew there wasn't time.

Candice was okay. No signs of injury, not even much fear, only a certain pain that Nevada could understand. Intellectually, she understood that it was an app, but the animal part of her only knew that it was walled off from Candice by this slim glass screen and couldn't get to her, no matter how close she seemed. And what could she say to make that even a little better?

"Hey," Nevada said, realizing she'd gone a whole ten seconds without speaking.

"Hey," Candice replied in a giggly copy of Nevada's American enunciation.

"Are you okay? Are you safe?"

Candice bit her lip in consternation for a telling moment but then nodded. "I'm… I'm good. They haven't hurt me. They need me."

"I know the feeling," Nevada said bitterly. "Doesn't last… Can you talk?" she asked, meaning could Candice speak freely.

Candice gave a microscopic shake of her head before answering. "Not for long. They'd throw me overboard."

Nevada nodded. So much for Candice giving her an address and asking to be given a ride to the airport. But in a way, it was a relief. She couldn't take Candice giving her a clue and being punished for it.

"What happened to your eye?" Candice asked.

"Didn't wear my safety goggles. Now I don't need them. Don't worry. We're coming to get you."

"We?"

"Yeah. I guess I'm bringing a one-legged man to an ass-kicking contest," Nevada realized.

"I have two legs," Butch protested. "One of them is metal, which makes it better."

Nevada pressed the phone to her chest. "I'm on the phone!" she shushed him.

Candice's face was serious when Nevada looked at her again. The formidable look of a lecture about to be given. Nevada cracked a grin. She'd even missed *that*.

"Listen to me, Thea. It's important. You can't come looking for me."

Nevada's grin froze. "Yeah, *right*."

"I'm serious. Singh has an army waiting for you."

"They can keep waiting," Nevada said, "in hell."

"This isn't a fight you can win. You don't stand a chance. You have to—you *need* to let me go. For me. I couldn't live with myself if something happened to you."

Nevada tried to laugh it off. "Well, how do you think I'd feel if something happened to me?"

"The last thing I want you to do is come all the way out here just to hear me nag. I hate to nag. Promise me you'll leave it until they let me go."

"And if they don't let you go?"

Candice winced; it took Nevada a moment to realize it was supposed to be a reassuring smile. "You've got a girl in every port, right? Find one of them instead. I'm not that special."

"You are." Nevada felt like her lungs were full of lead. She had to push past it with every breath. "Is Gore there?"

"Yeah."

"Put him on."

Candice turned her end of the transmission to Gore. His face was made for text messaging.

"Just so you know," Nevada told him, "if you harm one hair on her—"

"Hold that thought," Gore interrupted.

He turned the camera back on Candice. Nevada watched as his hand, dripping black, plucked a hair from her scalp.

"Dude, you can't just touch a black woman's hair."

The video stream shuddered as Gore shook the camera at Candice. "Say your goodbyes. We wouldn't want to keep Easy away from her busy schedule."

Candice gave the camera such a wounded look that Nevada couldn't believe it wasn't the same ache she felt. Like they were one and the same, bleeding from being cut right down the middle.

Candice coughed. "I won't say I don't have regrets, but meeting you could never be one of them."

Nevada pinched her lips together. It felt like there was another ton of lead in her chest, crushing down her lungs as she tried to breathe. "Candice… in case I never see you again… that one time we had to share a bed, you actually cuddled with me in your sleep and I wanted to wake you up and tease you about it, but I thought that would make you uncomfortable, so instead I slipped out of your spooning, and I planned to bring it up years later after we'd been intimate, but this seems like a good time too."

Candice looked askew for a moment, trying to untangle all that Nevada had babbled. Then she gave Nevada the sincerest smile she'd ever seen. "That actually sounds surprisingly considerate of you."

"Thanks, babe. You're my hero too."

"I wouldn't go that—"

The call ended, leaving only a black screen and the hum of a dial tone.

Nevada moved to smash the phone on the ground in a fit of frustration, but Butch smoothly relieved her of it before she could.

"No, no, I've got all my music on there. Let's not."

Nevada was left fuming, hands on her hips, with nothing to do but will Candice back to her, knowing all her energy, all her rage, wasn't doing anything no matter how fiercely she focused on it.

"So this girl, Candice—you're, like, dating her?" Butch asked.

"No. Shut up."

Butch slotted the phone into one of the many pockets in his khakis. “Okay, so if we rescue her and she ends up being really into me, you wouldn’t mind? You’d be maid of honor at our wedding?”

“Are you doing slam poetry right now? I don’t get what you’re saying at all.”

“Hey, it’s hard to meet people in your thirties. I can’t just join a roller derby team like you.”

“I can’t either. They banned me.” Nevada shook her head hard enough to throw off even the most resilient cobwebs. “I’m going to need a gun.”

“What happened to the last gun I gave you?”

“*Butch*—were you not just here for that?”

“Alright, alright already. We’ll consider it an early Christmas present.”

Butch led her to a wooden gun cabinet against the wall, so traditional it could’ve been Amish. On the top was a rack of rifles behind glass. Under that was a series of drawers. Butch pulled one open and took out a SIG Sauer P210.

He racked it to demonstrate it wasn’t loaded, then handed it to Nevada. She looked it over while he got magazines and ammo boxes from the same drawer. Walnut grip, stainless steel barrel, everything sleek and precision-made. She wouldn’t expect anything less from the Swiss.

“I really was going to give you this for Christmas,” Butch said. “So now don’t expect to get anything. Maybe a gift card. But that’s it.”

“It’s perfect,” Nevada said, taking a magazine from him and beginning to load it with shells from the box of 9mm Luger. “Now, when can we leave?”

“Leave? Easy, you haven’t slept, you haven’t eaten, you can’t wink, and you were in a plane crash.”

“If I weren’t, I’d just have jet lag.” Nevada loaded the full magazine into the P210, then tucked it into her waistband. She started loading another magazine.

“We can go in the morning. That’s when the meet’s set up. And that’s why you set up meets, so no one has to wait around reading Jack Reacher novels.”

“I like Jack Reacher.”

“Big surprise. Eat some pizza. Get some sleep. We’ll go first thing in the morning.”

"Why not go now?" Nevada asked. She felt snappish, irritable. Butch's phone started emitting a dial tone. The hum filled the air. If she said something about it, she'd probably seem ungrateful for the semiautomatic weapon. "We'll get there. I can sleep on the way. I can sleep while we're waiting for the meet… We can take the pizza with us."

Butch put a big hand on her shoulder. "This isn't a job interview. It's not going to make a difference how early we get there."

"You don't know that for sure."

"You're right. I don't know. I'm your stupid little brother who plays with Tonka toys. But if I thought it'd make any difference at all, do you really think I'd be standing here having this conversation with you? And not for nothing, but she did tell you no rescues…"

Nevada finished loading another magazine. She tucked it into a pocket. Butch's phone still hummed.

"That was all for Singh's benefit. She said she hates to nag. She *loves* to nag."

"So you *are* an item."

"Can you please turn your dial tone off before we discuss who I'm dating?"

Butch's brow furrowed. "Cell phones don't have dial tones."

The hum grew omnipresent before coming to a jarring end, shattering through the roof in a clatter of tiles, then smashing through the second floor and dropping into the living room with them. Nevada saw it for a split second, a swiftly landing meteor, and thought *mortar round* before it landed. Then everything was the explosion.

Emotions tangled up inside Candice, and one thought came to the forefront: she had never known how clichéd she was. Seeing Nevada again was like the sun breaking through a dark cloud, like a weight had been lifted off her shoulders, etc., et al. Nothing that would get her work as a poet.

But even if it wasn't original, there it was. Being reminded of Nevada's humor, her invincibility, even her goofy affection—it hoisted Candice's spirits as high as a chandelier.

Yes, she knew Nevada, knew the cool façade was half bullshit, but she didn't care. If Candice didn't want to give up all hope, she needed to believe in something. For all her flaws, Nevada was…Nevada. And thinking of Nevada unleashed on the likes of Singh and his minions allowed her a smile despite everything.

Talking to Nevada was such a relief that it took her a moment to feel Singh's attention pressing in on her. Gore stood stoic behind him, like a shadow in all but color. Candice made her face blank. She had to hide the sense of hope Nevada had given her, protect it, or it'd be snuffed out by how total their power over her was.

"Good talk? Good talk," Singh said. "You two are so cute together. Hashtag relationship goals. Now, about the skulls…"

Candice pushed past him. She felt Gore glowering at her, and Singh's sputtering reclamation of his dignity, as she headed for the Barcalounger and reclined on it. It was risky, it was careless—but what else could she do with Nevada's face behind her eyelids?

Candice talked with her hands, letting them gesture and run as she tried to put together in the real world what had made so much sense in her head. "I think the skulls want to be found. They want to be… turned on, for lack of a better word. And to do all… that, when they're a million years old—pardon the hyperbole—they're either magic, and there's no such thing as magic, or they're advanced technology. Technology we can't produce now. I don't know… Atlantis, time travelers, chariots of the gods. But it seems to me that the more advanced technology gets, the easier it is to use. Hold up an iPod next to a gramophone. So if they are some advanced technology, possibly even meant to be found by primitive civilizations, then it only stands to reason they'd be highly intuitive. That you could figure them out no matter the frame of reference. I think that's what they did. They gave off tachyons to tell us—what they need. That they need more if they're going to work. Like your phone telling you to plug it into a charger."

"Does that make sense to you?" Singh asked Gore. "It seems reasonable to me. Where can we get some tachyons?"

"I'll ask around," Gore said, stone-faced. Candice noted she had disappeared from his attention. His focus was solely on Singh, like a dog with a bone. "What about the girl?"

"Let's see if her theory pans out. If she's wrong, maybe she has a Plan B. If she's right—I don't know, it seems pretty tacky to kill her."

"She knows too much," Gore reminded him. Candice forced herself to stay quiet. She'd already gotten a stay of execution. She could only hope that was enough time for Nevada to find her.

"Yeah, yeah, that's too bad. I suppose we could just keep her." Singh let out a tiptoeing little laugh. "How much can it cost? A couple thousand a month? Drop in the bucket. And it's the right thing to do." He smiled at Candice. "How's that sound? You don't have to worry about rent anymore." Singh went back to Gore, lowering his voice so Candice couldn't hear except by straining her ears. "But hey, it's good you've got this aggressive energy, because it seems to me that if you're able to phone Nevada, you should be able to kill her too."

Gore nodded. "That's the plan."

The explosion flung Nevada aside like a child's toy that had fallen out of favor. The sudden acceleration blotted out her consciousness. Then she hit the floor hard enough for her bones to creak, the impact smashing wakefulness back into her.

Blood welled in her mouth. She spat and viscous red clung to her lips. She looked for Butch, but the power had cut out, casting the house into a darkness hellishly underscored by the scattered flames left by the blast. He was nowhere in sight, and smoke was filling the room, its acrid scent assaulting her nostrils. Everything felt numb to the touch, the slack in sensation that Nevada knew came with shock. She'd hurt when she had time to hurt.

"Butch!" she called.

"Stay *down*!" Butch yelled out of the darkness.

She looked around for him again, trying to find the source of his voice through only one eye. The open floor layout now seemed like an expanse she was lost in, a wasteland. But she made out her brother's bulky form. He'd landed on one of the couches.

Nevada belly-crawled to him as the mortars kept falling. She felt like she was inside a thundercloud or had thunder inside her. But her heart was already exploding, her blood was already lightning. Candice's voice had woken her up, keyed her into some secret frequency, and this bombing was only another stereo playing her tune.

She came to a stop beside Butch and drummed her hands on the floor. She was ready. She was fucking *ready*.

"Butch, you okay?"

"I can't feel my leg," Butch answered weepily.

Nevada sighed. "At least you haven't lost your sense of humor. You should try to."

Another mortar hit, and part of the ceiling caved in, dropping a baby grand piano through the floorboards.

"I didn't know you played," she said.

"Give me my gun back," Butch said.

"No takebacks. That's called Indian giving and it's considered very racially insensitive these days. I'm surprised at you."

Butch reached for the P210 in Nevada's waistband anyway. She slapped his hand away.

"Quit it! Get your own!"

"Maybe I will!" Butch retorted, peeking over the back of the couch to look to the gun cabinet. It was twenty-five feet away, with the glass blown out by the pressure waves, but still had enough firepower to survive a weekend in Chicago.

He started to get up. Nevada pressed him back down, and another mortar hit, this time elsewhere in the house. They were inside a dollhouse being sledgehammered from the outside.

"I'll get it," she said grudgingly.

"Why should you go?" Butch challenged.

"Because you only have one leg," Nevada said, reaching down to rap her knuckles on his prosthetic.

"Exactly, I'm less vulnerable. Anyone shoots you anywhere, you're screwed."

"The robot leg isn't going to help you if you get blown apart, genius."

"Yeah, well, my house, my rules."

"I have a counterargument," Nevada said, and overturned the couch so that Butch was pinned under it.

She sprinted for the gun cabinet. The space between it and her seemed to stretch instead of letting her get close to it. Another mortar went off with a bass growl thick enough to drown in. The explosion ripped through the façade of the house and showered Nevada with what was left. Debris scratched and smashed at her flesh like she was struggling through a briar patch—all she could do was shield her face and keep moving.

The gun cabinet loomed in front of her like a punch being thrown at her face. Nevada threw herself down, sliding on her hip until the cabinet stopped her. Immediately she popped up, throwing open the shattered glass door and grabbing for a long gun. She pulled down a Model 89 .500 S&W Magnum Lever Action—a rifle that fired bullets about the size of her thumb.

She wasn't sure about firing it without breaking her collarbone, much less being able to hit anything after the first round, but it'd be just right for Butch. After he'd had the audacity to grow up taller than her, she might as well put his Bigfoot status to good use.

Another mortar hit in the neighboring room. It blew out the wall, splashing disintegrated plaster across the floor, leaving broken pipes and disemboweled wiring hanging in space like viscera. The gun cabinet shielded Nevada from the blast; it also toppled over on top of her, smashing her to the ground. Something popped in her chest, letting in jagged pain.

"Easy!" Butch called. He'd worked himself out from under the couch and now leapt up to run to her, but just as he broke into a sprint, he had to come to a skidding stop.

A blinding LED spotlight scythed through the front door, long since blown off its hinges, and lit up the space between him and Nevada. Enough light backwashed from the spotlight to show the jeep it was attached to, stopped in the mansion's front yard with a mounted machine gun aimed inside.

"Butch! *Psst!*" Nevada said in a forceful whisper. She held up the Model 89 rifle. "You keep this loaded?"

"Only when you're in town!" Butch whispered back.

Nevada took firm hold of the Model 89, marshalled her strength, and slid it across the floor to Butch. He scooped it up, ducking behind the cover of the overturned couch as the spotlight's beam rolled to the left and bleached everything around Nevada almost to a pure white but didn't see her so close to the ground. It roamed to the right, pushing through windows and holes in the wall like a giant arm reaching for Butch.

He clutched the Model 89 to his chest and stayed low behind the couch. The spotlight thrust their combined shadow into the wall. He was lost in the darkness that welled up where the light couldn't get through.

The light shut off with a muted squeal of cooling electronics. The silence and darkness were leavened only by the small, scattered flames crackling away. Nevada saw Butch's big outline backed against the couch. He started for her, but she held up a hand. He froze.

The machine gun opened fire, bullets shredding through the wall and windows, pouring into the room. They swept across the house in an endless stream, crossing the gun cabinet holding Nevada down—she twisted her head to the side and closed her eyes as the bullets cracked into the cabinet. Wooden splinters spat out of the impacts, spraying into her face. Then the bullets passed on. Nevada wiped her face and opened her eyes.

Butch was pressed belly-low to the floor, using what little cover the couch provided. The bullets hacked into it, a swarm of axes stuffing flying out like confetti. They continued on to tear through the right side of the house. By the time it stopped, the entire house had been hosed down with thousands of rounds. Nevada imagined she'd be able to hear the spent shells clinking together in a knee-high hill if she weren't deafened by the shooting. Her ears rang like church bells.

Her hearing slowly came back, and as the seconds dragged on, she was able to hear someone talking. "*Gee, Butch, you haven't sorted your DVD collection*," Butch whined in a falsetto voice. "Maybe because you come over, the house blows up. Ever think about that?"

"It's not that bad," Nevada said. "A little paint, some flowers…"

"Can I just shoot them all now?" Butch spat.

"Plans like that are why I make the plans."

"Great; what's your plan?"

"I'm working on it."

"Take your time."

"Thinking about plans for more than five seconds is also why I make the plans."

"We don't have more than five seconds."

Car doors slammed with a brusque chop. Whoever was in the jeep was getting out of it. A raid, sweeping the mansion room by room to make sure they were down.

Nevada inhaled. Something hit her—a tart scent. She sniffed. Leaking gas line. It must've been damaged in the onslaught. She looked around for it. "Butch, got a light?"

Butch dug into his pocket, coming up with a Zippo lighter. "I'm down to two a day, you know."

Nevada gestured impatiently for it. He sent it skittering across the floor. She slapped her hand down onto it, listening for where the gas was seeping out. That and light footsteps, barely rising above the sound of the small fires frittering away.

They were coming in through the front door, not that she could see them with so little light. No flashlights, so they had to be using night vision. Nevada flicked the wheel on the lighter. It sparked but refused to light. She heard Butch slowly work the lever action on the Model 89, chambering a round.

"Easy," he hissed warningly.

She ignored him. He wouldn't go against her—not when it mattered. She flicked the wheel again. Heard boots crunching bits of glass underfoot. Close now. Inside the room. She gripped the P210 Butch had given her with her other hand. The lighter caught. A little supernova in her hand. Nevada felt the attention of everyone in the room on her like a hand clamping down on her shoulder. She threw the lighter, shifted the gun to her right hand, and shut her eyes.

Through her closed eyelids, the burst of flame as the lighter hit the gas pipe looked like someone throwing a bucket of red paint on the speckled black of her blindness. She opened her eyes to the hellish red of the lit-up world and pivoted to fire on the gunmen, but Butch beat her to it, stepping out of cover to fire the Model 89. The thing was a cannon, its blast a focused version of the mortars that had just gone off.

The first round took a gunman in the chest, punching through his body armor, a burst of blood redder than red as he flew back. The second gunman got it in the face, somersaulting back before Nevada could catch more than a glimpse of what the half-inch-thick bullet did to his face. The third gunman got a shot off; it sparked against Butch's artificial leg and pinged away.

"Prick!" Butch swore, pumping the lever action and firing his own shot into the man's thigh. It bit into the flesh like a rabid dog. "How do you like it?"

Nevada mentally counted: driver, passenger, two in the backseat. That left one. And anyone who had shown up for the first day of class on small-unit tactics would send *someone* around back to flank. She scanned the room and saw a shuttered window jostling as the gunman pushed aside the blinds for a clear shot.

Nevada drew on him and fired half her clip through the Persian blinds. After four bullets clawed their way through him, he slumped forward, tangled in the blinds like a fly in a spider's web.

Butch came to get her, slinging the Model 89 on his shoulder before lifting the gun cabinet. The blown gas pipe had become an angry hive of fire swarming up the ceiling. "That's good. Don't just blow my house up, set it on fire too."

"You're welcome," Nevada told him, slithering out from under the cabinet.

Butch helped pull her to her feet before dropping it. "I should probably check if this place had insurance."

"Ya think?"

She made a beeline for the gunman Butch had hobbled, an Afrikaner who was pulling a tourniquet around his thigh. Seeing them coming, he went for his gun. Nevada already had hers trained on him. "Don't you think you have enough orifices by now?"

He dropped the weapon. She kicked it away and crouched down next to him. Holstered the P210 and tightened his tourniquet for him.

"I hear that torture doesn't work, so let's just use the honor system. Any other guys out there?"

He shook his head and spoke with a South African accent so thick it could've been wearing clogs. "Just us. Small crew. Short notice."

Butch let out a moan. Nevada turned to look at him. His DVD collection had taken a direct hit from a mortar. Where he was standing, it looked like someone had committed a hate crime against a Redbox.

"It would be one thing if I hadn't upgraded," he said miserably, "but I had some Blu-rays in there. Even 4K discs!"

A *Scarface* DVD had landed near Nevada. She picked it up and showed it to him. "Hey, you can still be a big hit back at the dorm."

"Real funny. What's your favorite movie? *Princess Diaries*? *Legally Blonde*? Something else written entirely for thirteen-year-old girls?"

Nevada looked back at the Afrikaner. "You can see what I have to deal with; I'm not in a great mood. Who hired you?"

"John Gore."

She nodded. "You know where he is?"

"No."

"You sure?" she asked and banged her hand on his wound. He cried out, the usual sobbing and sniveling and dry heaves.

"I'm sure!"

"I guess torture isn't reliable. Kind of entertaining, but—listen, I want you to deliver a message for me. Can you do that?"

He nodded, lips pressed tightly together against the pain.

"'Course you can do that," Nevada continued. "It's not like I'm asking you to deliver a Riverdance for me. Tell Gore that I'm coming for him, I'm going to kill him, and I'm going to—oh, let's see—rip his heart out, dip it in chocolate, and eat it. Has that been done?"

"Don't micromanage," Butch cautioned.

Nevada snapped her fingers. "When you're right, you're right." She looked back at the Afrikaner. "I'm gonna give you some creative freedom there. Come up with something good. Rip his head off, shit down his throat, you know, that kinda thing. Be creative. Think you can manage that?"

"*Ja, ja*!"

"You're being real cool for a white guy in South Africa. You're way over on the Charlize Theron side of the spectrum. Hey, say 'diplomatic immunity.' Just once."

The Afrikaner looked at her in confusion. "Diplomatic immunity?"

"It's just been revoked!" Butch cried. He fired the Model 89.

At close range, it did things to the Afrikaner's head that usually happened to pumpkins after Halloween.

Nevada wiped her face off. "Butch," she said slowly, "what was that?"

"*Lethal Weapon 2*," Butch told her. "Number 3 was the one with Rene Russo."

"I know which Lethal Weapon it was! What happened to 'I need you to send a message'?"

Butch gestured vaguely. "I thought it was like—when you get to hell, tell Gore… da da da da…"

"No! He's not dead! We still need to kill him!" Nevada spat. "I got some on my lip!"

"Yeah, nobody told me that. But maybe we could leave a note."

"It's not really the same thing, is it?" Nevada looked down. "And now I need a new shirt. There's brain all over this one."

"I can get another one out of my go-bag. Which I should probably get before the house burns down. So thanks for that."

"Oh, you're homeless now? That'll go well with the *psychosis*!"

"You shouldn't make fun of mental illness. It's not woke."

Nevada kneaded her sinuses. "Just get the go-bag. Without any homicides, please?"

"No promises!" Butch snarled as he stomped off.

"This is why Mom likes me best," Nevada muttered to herself.

CHAPTER 11

THE LIGHTS WERE OFF IN the hold of the *Liparus*. To Gore, the vast, empty expanse gave the darkness an added quality, a realness and a texture that made the lights on the elevator he rode down feel like a beachhead in hostile territory. One being inexorably beaten back.

With the track finished and the workers back in their quarters, the only other light was the circle of work lamps shining on the isolation chamber. In the darkness, it was like a pool of frozen amber on an endless black setting. Singh stood on the edge of the light, so far back that he was only an outline. It took many steps, as Gore walked up, before there was something to him.

"You should be sleeping," Gore said.

"Who sleeps on Christmas Eve?" Singh replied. "Not that I'd know, my family didn't celebrate Christmas, but you get the gist. Who can sleep when you want something you don't have?"

He finally pulled himself away from the sight of the illuminated chamber—a wan, colorless imitation of what had been when the skulls were active—to look at Gore.

"How about those tachyons?"

Gore took his tablet out from under his arm, consulting it just to make sure there'd been no last-minute changes. There weren't. "Our procurer has the emitter. It'll be a week."

"And the payload?" Singh asked the question like he was quizzing Gore.

"It's ready now. We're good to go."

"That is great! Wonderful news! I assume we'll have our privacy."

"International waters in the Somali Sea," Gore said. "We're underway now. No one will bother us there."

"And Nevada?" Singh pressed.

"A team went in. Private contractors, four-man fire team. They hammered the target with mortar rounds, then breached the compound."

"And?"

"We lost contact with them."

Singh snatched the tablet from him and threw it against the isolation chamber. "How hard can it be to kill someone? People die *by accident* every day! I just watched the nine o'clock news—people are dying from laundry detergent. *How are you less deadly than laundry detergent*!?" He ran his hands over his face, clearing away the sudden sweat that had washed over his features. "Alright. Okay. Has another team gone in, or do we have to pay more for that?"

"The firm sent in another team. The place was empty." Gore shrugged. "Well, bodies."

With flattened hands, Singh chopped the air in front of him into distinct segments. "Track her. Find her. Kill her. I don't care how you do it. I don't care what it costs. I used to pay her less than I spent on my playlist guru, so how good can she be? Find the bitch!"

"That won't be a problem."

"Oh really?" Singh spat. "Because lately that seems to have been a big problem for you. Shaq has free throws and you have Easy Nevada."

Gore bristled. With a certain sadistic joy, he put in, "She left a note with the bodies. It says, and I quote, 'We're coming to get you, X-O-X-O.'"

Singh sucked in air. "Anything else?"

"The 'i' was dotted with a little heart. I could show you a picture if you hadn't smashed my tablet."

Singh put his hands on Gore's shoulders. It took most of his reach. "Well then, that simplifies things. What more does she have to do, load the bullets into the gun for you? Shoot her, stab her, I don't care. I want her to bleed and die. *No*!" Singh said with sudden vehemence, his voice echoing through the black on all sides. "No. I want her alive. Even if it's just alive enough to watch me kill the Cushing woman in front of her. Then she dies. They both die."

"I'll see what I can do," Gore promised.

"Good man. Good." Singh let go of him. "She has no right to stress me out the way she is. I am under enough pressure already. I am an entrepreneur. I am a job creator. 'We're coming to get you.' Who expresses herself like that? It's a death threat, that's what it is. That's where we're at now. She's sending death threats. Totally uncool."

"Would you like some Benzedrine?"

"Yes, please."

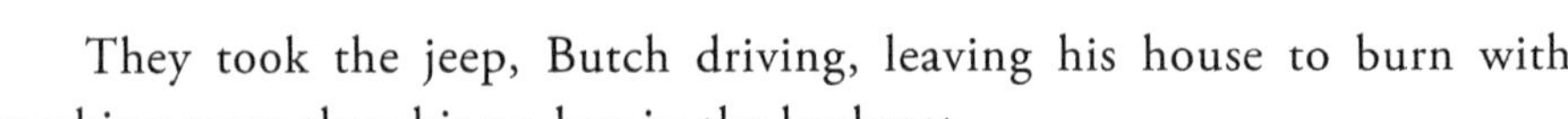

They took the jeep, Butch driving, leaving his house to burn with nothing more than his go-bag in the backseat.

"Do you think we should call someone?" Nevada asked. She was now wearing bootleg Gulf War merchandise—a shirt of Bart Simpson in desert camo and a gas mask, saying *Go ahead, Hussein, have a cow.*

"Call who?"

"I don't know. The Bandar still think you're a god. What's going to happen when they find out your house burned down? Maybe we should let someone know that there's a bunch of Pygmies whose belief system just took a lead pipe to the head."

Butch waved dismissively. "If they turn into a bunch of atheists, I'm pretty sure they'll let people know themselves."

Nevada slid back against her headrest, watching the headlights bring the road ahead out of the darkness as the shocks struggled with the bumpy path they were navigating. It felt horribly circular for a moment: more driving through the night, more desperate scurries that she could only hope were bringing her closer to Candice. But there was a solidness to having Butch with her. She reached out and put her hand on his wrist as he worked the stick shift. He didn't shake it off, even if it meant staying in second gear until she took her hand back.

The strange thing was, now that they were in motion, Nevada felt like she could relax. Even if Butch's driving was objectively terrifying. She didn't sleep, but she did lean her head back until she was nearly comfortable as she explained everything to Butch. He knew the basics: her son, the job, Singh, the skulls. Current events required some explanation, even to her. She skimmed over Candice, Sudan, South Sudan, the crash, until she was sure Butch was about as informed as he was ever going to get.

"Let me get this straight," Butch said. With Nevada resting her eyes in the middle of the night, his voice came out of darkness. "First you had this Farouq guy to worry about. He's dead."

"Murder on the Orient Express, you might say," Nevada quipped.

"Don't be racist. But his father, Nazir, then he was after you. But he's dead too now."

"Unless he managed to hitch a ride at twenty thousand feet."

"So now there's Singh, your old boss, who has turned on you, and he also hired Farouq in the first place. But that's it? He's the big bad guy."

"Uh-huh."

"That's your third bad guy," Butch said. "At this point I'm expecting Thanos to be behind it all. Although I suppose if he was, we'd just start grabbing up Infinity Gems to ruin his day."

"Is that a veiled criticism I sense?" Nevada asked.

"Just that we're going to an awful lot of trouble to rescue some girl. This isn't China, y'know. There are others out there. You ever try Tinder? Every stand-up special I've seen has had jokes about Tinder. And if stand-up comedians are getting dates, you should have no problem."

Nevada didn't take the bait. She heard Butch start to say something about J-date, but he was interrupted by a dream about dogs. She would've preferred to dream about Candice again, but on the bright side, at least the dogs weren't at a strip club.

When she woke up, it was like an epoch had passed. The jungle was gone along with the night. In the cold light of day, a port city had sprung up all around the jeep, which was parked outside a harbor, the smell of seawater seasoning the air as waves licked placidly at the shore.

Nevada righted herself, snapping the kinks out of her neck, popping them out of her knuckles. There was no sign of Butch, but she couldn't imagine he'd be gone long. She hoped not. Nevada never knew quite what she was getting with her brother, where he'd be when she picked up with him. It was like playing slots. Sometimes the three cherries lined up and he was all there. Sometimes...

Nevada took a deep breath, centering herself, letting the sea air work its way through her lungs and back out of her. Above, seagulls brayed, battling the wind into a state of equilibrium that looked like they were standing still. She thought of Jacques, so much like *The Flying Carpet* that he could've been a part of it, always reliable, always there for her—until now. She missed him, but she didn't have time to miss him. She barely had time to take another breath and let the salty air tingle on her taste buds.

This might be the last time she saw the sea. Or, given the boat, the last time she saw dry land.

Nevada shook her head. Business as usual. She wasn't allowed to die until the job was done.

Butch appeared and dropped a paper bag onto the hood of the jeep. "Bunny chow!" He took out two foil-topped metal containers, tossed one into Nevada's lap, and then brought out shrink-wrapped plastic utensils for both of them.

"If that's a new nickname for me..." Nevada began threateningly.

Butch peeled the foil off the top of his container. Inside was a hollowed out chunk of bread with curry filling it out. "It's breakfast. I thought we'd eat before we set sail. Speaking of." He slammed a bottle of Dramamine onto the hood. "Don't say I never gave you nothing."

"I would never say that. You gave me lice that one time."

Butch grinned bemusedly. "I'll never understand how you can get seasick on a boat—a nice, sturdy boat—but on that old crate Jacques flew, you're fine. Your body must be an idiot."

Given some of the people that her body had singled out for extended personal relationships, Nevada couldn't argue. At least, not about that. "Since we're calling your boat 'nice' and 'sturdy,' I'm assuming you got rid of that antique of yours?"

"Hell no. She's a classic."

"It's a PT boat," Nevada countered. She looked around the harbor, finally spotting the old gunmetal-gray tub at one of the moorings. Butch had kept it more or less spotless, but nevertheless, it managed to give a psychic impression of rust. The eighty-foot Elco-class ship had had all its armaments removed, which was almost enough to restore Nevada's faith in government, but Butch had personally installed a harpoon gun on the prow. In case, Nevada supposed, he ever ran into Moby Dick.

Nevada ate. The moment the food touched her lips, she realized how ravenous she was. It tasted good too, the bread offsetting the spiciness of the curry, like saltine crackers in five-alarm chili. She could only pull herself away to razz Butch a little more.

"You know, for what you've spent to keep that thing running all these years, you probably could've bought a yacht."

"I wouldn't enjoy a yacht as much," Butch replied guilelessly. "And she has a name."

Nevada looked at the bow of the ship. *Blue Lagoon* was written in obscenely proud letters, straight and tall and perfectly proportioned. God help her, he'd probably paid someone a fortune to do that too. "You need to think up a better name."

"Why? It reminds me of my lifelong ambition."

"What's that?" Nevada asked, already regretful.

"Get reincarnated as Brooke Shields's wig."

Nevada grimaced and dusted off the crumbs of the bunny chow. "Let's just go. We can talk on the way."

"Fine by me." Butch took the empty takeaway container from her and stuffed it into the bag it'd come in. "You mind steering? I need to catch some shuteye."

"Why not?" Nevada swung herself out of the jeep, old wounds coming back to life. She promised herself that she wouldn't do any calisthenics for a while. Just have a nice sit and steer the boat. By the time she found Singh, she'd be well enough to vomit on him.

Butch crumpled the paper bag and tossed it into the backseat of the jeep, replacing it with the go-bag, which he slung over his shoulder. Nevada circled her right arm, trying to work the stiffness of being slept on out as she walked with him toward the *Blue Lagoon*.

She glanced back at the jeep. Butch had parked in a handicapped spot. "Someone's gonna tow that thing."

"Another blow dealt to the forces of evil," Butch told her.

Butch had already charted a course for her at the *Blue Lagoon*'s helm. They were traveling a good eight hundred miles to Madagascar. At fifty miles per hour, it'd be the better part of a day before they even hit the shore. And she'd need to refuel after twelve hours. Butch had replaced the boat's two Mark 13 torpedoes with big fuel tanks to increase its range, but she'd never seen him tap them yet without it getting messy. At least he'd installed a big sound system to go with it. Though that still left Butch's taste in music.

Many, *many* repetitions of John Denver later, Butch emerged from the crew quarters. Nevada checked her watch. Ten hours. She didn't know how he did it. Did he wake up, then bang his head against the wall until he went back to sleep?

Butch went to what had once been the chart house and opened up the refrigerator he'd installed there, taking out a water bottle and draining it in one gulp. He dropped the empty plastic into a recycling bin. Unlike the series of bachelor pads he took over when he came ashore, Butch kept the *Blue Lagoon* fastidiously tidy. Nevada could only imagine he'd realized that if he let the garbage pile up too much, the boat would sink.

"Hey," he said. He hadn't bothered to put his prosthetic back on—there wasn't a lot of walking to be done on a PT boat. Instead, he marched around with a crutch under one arm. Nevada resolutely avoided making the pirate joke he clearly wanted her to go for. "I've been thinking."

"That is news," Nevada quipped.

"E-he-he," Butch mock-laughed, dropping like a stone into a gunnery station that had once held twin Browning .50 caliber machine guns. "This whole meshuggeneh—you, Candice, Singh, Blood—"

"Gore," Nevada corrected. "It's not that hard to keep track of," she added defensively.

Butch put up his leg and his stump on the side of the "bucket" that held his seat. "Yeah, yeah. Here's what I'm thinking: movie deal. We get to Hollywood, sell the rights to your life story, we're set for life."

"I already sold the rights," Nevada said. When she caught sight of the stencil line tattoo around his stump, it now struck her as kinda funny. She had to be getting loopy.

"You did?"

"Yeah. Went through a lot of rewrites though. Ended up as a Dora the Explorer movie."

"No one noticed that a Dora the Explorer movie was full of murder and alcohol abuse?"

Nevada rolled her shoulders. "No one noticed that all the old hard-R movies are now full of life lessons and the power of friendship, so… Hey, you wanna take over? My wrists are cramping."

Butch hopped over to take her place at the wheel. "That must be rough for a lesbian. I mean, a guy can take Viagra—"

"Butch, I'm not Sting. I don't take ten hours to get a woman off."

"Speaking of the female orgasm…"

"Too easy," Nevada said, dropping down into the gunnery station Butch had just vacated. She put her feet up.

"We're doing all this to save your friend, Candice, right? I have friends. Not sure how many I'd storm the castle for."

Nevada worried the inside of her lip between her teeth, then coached her face into a tight-lipped smile. As the silence wore on, Butch grunted, dismissing the topic. He knew when to let something alone, but however comfortable he was with the unsaid, Nevada wasn't. She dragged her hands over her face before finally replying.

"I don't know what I am to her."

"Okay. What's she to you?"

Nevada got up, bouncing on her heels a few times. "The face that launched one old rust bucket."

"Not rusty," Butch corrected.

"You know, there's something Jacques said to me—I've been in love, but I've never been the first person to say it. But if I don't say it, I'm not touching it. And if I'm not touching it, then I don't know if it's not there."

Butch glanced at her. He had the doleful eyes of a dog: not exactly understanding, but always commiserating. "Well, if it's not there, she's an idiot."

Nevada smiled. "Thanks."

"Hey, I'm your brother. I have to love you. But if you can find someone who *chooses* to—"

"Don't make me throw something at you. I might miss and put a hole in this thing."

"It's a warship."

Nevada leaned against the radio mast. "It's wood."

"Mahogany."

Nevada let him have it. It seemed important to him.

She stared out at the waves, the clouds, the horizon, wishing Candice was there to see them with her. It was a bone-deep fixation. Couldn't fight it, didn't want to. Wherever Candice was, she'd either leave with her or not at all.

Butch's voice rang out, a little singsong: "I spy with my little eye something beginning with *O*."

"Ocean."

"I spy with my little eye something beginning with *S*."

"Sea."

"I spy with my little eye something *else* that starts with the letter *S*."

"Saltwater."

"You've played this game before."

CHAPTER 12

NEVADA CAUGHT SOME SHUT-EYE BEFORE they arrived at Madagascar. It didn't leave her feeling particularly rested, but it did let her skip a few hours. It seemed like she blinked and they were weighing anchor by a Malagasy fishing village. Nevada took some 101-proof painkiller and ate a power bar.

Wooden canoes came out to take them to shore, in hopes of getting the business that Butch was happy to give them. He paid a fat stack of bills for the *Blue Lagoon* to go untouched while he was gone, promising another helping from his money belt if gas for a refueling was there when he got back. He also paid for transportation—a pair of bicycles for their fifty-mile trip to Tsingy de Bemaraha National Park. He overpaid for both, but as he told Nevada, it was enough for the fishers to feed their families for months.

"Chinese boats come down here, overfish the waters, and the guys with diving masks and fishing nets are left with nothing to eat. Colonialism didn't end for these people, it just got outsourced," Butch said.

Nevada jutted out her chin, both angry and bitter at the fact that nothing could be done, a little mad at herself that bitterness outweighed righteous anger. *I've been spending too much time with Candice*, she said to herself and instantly crushed the thought down as hard as she could. She looked at Butch instead.

"Sorry I yelled at you," she said.

Butch grinned in acknowledgment. "What, we're pretending I don't usually deserve it?"

It was three hours to Tsingy, with nothing to do but pedal and make conversation with Butch, whom she loved but was realistic about. It made Nevada think about how lucky Dora the Explorer and all other movie characters were. If nothing was happening, the director said "cut," the projectionist changed the reel, and it was on to the next exciting scene. No one went to a theater to see Tom Cruise sitting in traffic or James Bond filling out the paperwork that got him his Aston-Martin DB5. But the clock hands in her world maintained their inexorable pace, just as the miles between her and Candice refused to get out of the way.

For the last few miles, they rode in the dark, with only the sputtering, motion-powered headlamps lighting the way. They picked up the lights of their destination in the distance, a French colonial bungalow that could be seen for miles. "That's where we're meeting your contact?" Nevada asked.

"Yeah. No. That's where we 'await further instructions.'"

"Does he have information on Singh or not?"

"Do you have somewhere else to be?" Butch retorted.

"Don't answer a question with a question. What do you think this is, a J.J. Abrams show?"

They pulled to a stop in front of the bungalow. Butch led off with his real foot, letting the bike fall where it fell, but he stumbled. Nevada, her own dismount much smoother, grabbed his sleeve and held him up as he righted himself. Her thighs were throbbing, her whole lower body radiating with the tension of muscular exhaustion. She could only imagine how it was for Butch, his stump having to grind against the prosthetic to do anything.

"Yeah," Butch said by way of thanks, brushing her hand off, and they went inside.

There was an envelope lying on the welcome mat. Nevada stooped to pick it up before Butch could go for it. She read it quickly, her brother hovering over her shoulder.

"They thought we'd be here early, but they won't make it until morning. Relax and enjoy the lodgings."

The bungalow was one big room, with beds against the wall. They ate something Nevada forgot as soon as she swallowed, then laid down. Listening to Butch breathe in the dark reminded Nevada of being a kid. Bunk beds and glow-in-the-dark stars.

She fingered her eyepatch, trying to adjust it to be comfortable enough to sleep in. The sooner she took it off, the sooner she'd have to rely on Butch to patch her up again. She preferred to heal as much as possible before then.

Butch's voice drifted to her. "Can we talk?"

"Sure," Nevada answered. "What do you want to talk about?"

"I don't know—how about the Avengers Initiative?"

"Fuck off."

Sleep went into Nevada like a knife between the ribs. It bled back out of her in dreams she couldn't remember.

When she woke up, breakfast was three power bars. Butch had found a pamphlet and was reading from it. "Get this: Tsingy is a Malagasy word meaning 'where you cannot walk barefoot.' All that rock is razor sharp. Eats through shoes with every minute you walk on it."

"Just what I need," Nevada said with her mouth full. "An excuse to go shoe shopping." Chewing, she looked out the window. The landscape was a stone forest with jagged towers of limestone stabbing up into the air. It looked like some gothic cathedral halfway ravaged by time, still holding onto its grandeur even in ruins. A destroyed fortress of six hundred miles, its canyons and caves tantalizingly impassible.

"Two hundred million years ago, calcite formed into thick limestone at the bottom of a pond or lake. Later tectonic activity brought the limestone to the surface, the sea level fell during an ice age, and monsoon rains washed away the soft rock to leave only something called *karst*. Then groundwater—"

"What are you," Nevada interrupted, "the tour guide?"

Butch tucked away the pamphlet and looked out at the jagged columns of stone that formed a maze of razors. "I gotta admit, I would never see this kind of shit if I weren't with you."

Fresh clothes and climbing gear had been set by the back door. Thick jackets and trousers, work gloves, and hiking boots. Nevada wasn't surprised to find that they fit perfectly. Everyone in Singh's world seemed to have resources and abilities that were nearly unimaginable; why should his enemies be any different?

"Easy, think the rest of the tour is here."

Nevada looked up. She hadn't registered any movement, any noise, but a tall black man in military fatigues stood on an outcropping of rock twenty feet from the bungalow. Yards away stood another man in the same dress. They were both armed with M4 carbines in what looked like good condition.

She picked up others in the tall grass that led back the way they had come, and she'd stake at least a twenty that there were others she couldn't see. They were making no move to advance. They just stood there, like buzzards.

"Maybe they want their hiking shit back," Butch suggested.

Someone knocked at the front door. Nevada gave Butch a quick hand signal—*stay put*—and went to answer it. Another black man. His lips had been cut away, exposing all of his gums, his teeth seeming to bulge out from the rimless opening in a grotesque smile. His ears were slashed off as well, leaving only holes wrapped in scar tissue.

"Easy Nevada," the man said. He sounded garbled, but after a moment, Nevada realized it was the other way around. With no lips to form the words, they came straight off his tongue, crude, unrefined. Harsh.

At her waist, Nevada held out a hand, reassuring Butch to stand down. "Yes?"

"Follow me. I will take you the rest of the way."

She followed him to the back door. Butch made a face asking for an explanation, but before she could say anything, a lemur jumped onto a nearby windowsill. Butch nearly shot it.

"God! Fuck off, Zoboomafoo..."

Their guide led them through the labyrinth of gray stone. Across high ledges, up rickety ladders, through caves so narrow they had to turn and sidestep through the alleys of tight space or go on all fours to keep under the low ceiling. The limestone that surrounded them lived up to its reputation, ripping and tearing into clothes, boots, skin if they weren't careful. Even Butch's prosthetic leg showed wear and tear after the first hour of travel.

"You know, Easy, normally I try to get along with your friends, but when they don't have lips, well, I start to worry..."

"They're called the Zuni," Nevada said, carefully picking her steps on the way up a slope. "Somewhere between a cult and a fucked-up tribe. Those scars are how they initiate new members."

"Geez. And I thought circumcision was bad."

"We've had a few run-ins. I think they're after the same skulls Singh wants."

"And back when you were getting the skulls for Singh, I suppose you had a friendly but overall respectful rivalry with them?"

"You know how good I am at showing respect."

"So, one more group of people out to kill you. It's amazing. Africa has thousands of different cultures and ethnicities, and yet they can all agree on your murder."

"Maybe I should do something with my hair," Nevada quipped.

They moved through *grikes*—ruler-straight rows of serrated stone that had once been caves before the roofs collapsed, leaving only the walls. The one they were in led steadily upward. The slope was so steep that they had to hook carabiners onto a metal cable and pull themselves up, hand over hand, until they were on top of a knife-edged plateau.

Nevada could see the bed of nails continue for miles, in all directions now, surrounding them. There was no soil this high, only aloe and euphorbia, their roots seeming frozen in the act of lashing the rock as they cast downward in search of water.

Two more Zuni vultures waited for them, guns at the ready. On the ground sat a man wrapped in bandages, swaddled in them, and something about him struck Nevada as familiar, even though it was obviously impossible for her to recognize him.

"Let me guess," Butch said, eying the bandaged man. "He starts laughing, takes all that shit off, turns out to be invisible, right?"

Nevada heaved a sigh. "We've all seen James Whale's classic The Invisible Man with Claude Rains, Butch!"

Their guide was in no mood for banter. "Leave your weapons here. The man may have the information he requested—all of Mr. Singh's off-shore accounts and expenditures—and Miss, the Lady is waiting for you there."

Nevada followed his hand. A rope bridge led off the plateau, onto a finger, a *needle*, of towering rock. On the top of it, impossibly, a hut had been built. There was barely a foot of clearance between its walls and the edge of the rock it sat on. Fetishes marked the dark windows. Cracked tortoise shells, fractured horns, jagged tusks. Dead animals twisted together with plant matter into inscrutable knots. It was like an evolution of the aesthetic that had left the Zuni men without ears or lips.

"Uh-uh," Butch said. "She's not going in there."

"The Lady wishes to do Ms. Nevada a reading." There was a smile in the guide's voice. It gave the unsettling impression that, with the skin peeled back from his jaws, he was *always* smiling. “This is the price for the Lady’s help. We do not give you this knowledge for free.”

“It’s okay, Butch.” Nevada slowly drew her P210 and stooped to set it down on the rock. “You find Candice. I’ll be right back.”

“Find…” Butch stopped, interrupted by one of the Zuni handing a tablet to him. He looked it over. “Jesus, okay. We’re not talking about Singh leaving the money he gets from his lemonade stand off his tax returns. This guy’s into drugs, guns—other drugs…”

“A boat,” Nevada said, speaking more from a flash of insight than any logic. Like Candice had managed to beam a thought to her through some unspoken connection.

“What?”

“Candice said they would throw her overboard. That’s got to be it. She’s on a boat, she was trying to tell me—and she says I never listen.”

“Okay, a boat, I’ll look into that. Now please step back from the African Chainsaw Massacre house.”

“I’ll be fine,” Nevada assured him. “Trust me.”

“That bridge looks like Noah built it as a warm-up for the Ark.”

Nevada looked down at the rotting planks that made up the rope bridge. They did not inspire confidence. “You’re just applying Eurocentric Western standards to the innovative construction techniques of indigenous—”

She stepped on the first plank. It gave way, dropping her until she caught herself on the hand ropes, which strained and frayed in her grip. Nevada pulled herself back up and set her foot on the next plank. This one held.

“And that is how you *test* a plank on a rope bridge to make sure it can hold your weight.”

“Uh-huh.” Butch noticed a Zuni hovering over his shoulder, keeping a close eye on him. “Hey, ever think about growing a beard?”

Nevada walked across the swaying bridge, carefully testing each plank before putting her weight on it. Almost all of them groaned threateningly, but no more broke. Their shudders as her weight fell on them echoed down into the grikes below and were answered by fruit bats and parrots. Shrieks and cackles.

Nevada ignored them. She inched forward, every step creaking, groaning, the ropes so frayed they seemed insubstantial in her hands. When the wind picked up, sweeping the bridge to the side and then letting it fall back, the whole construction wheezed as a dying animal would—ropes straining, planks rattling against each other like dry bones. Nevada forced herself on.

Her hands caressed the posts on the other side at last, feeling the sturdy wooden stakes that held the ropes in place. Nevada squeezed them for a moment, reassuring herself that they hadn't been as flimsy as they'd felt. It was a long moment.

"I've felt you." The voice came from inside the hut, feminine, singsong, a mélange of accents: Zambia, the Congo, Nigeria, even the Caribbean. Nevada couldn't place what came first. "So shy, so cautious… so unwilling to submit to the inevitable. But always drawing closer, as a fish nibbles at the worm before it bites. And now, here you are. Thea Quatermain."

Nevada rounded the hut. The pillar it stood on had been eaten away at like an apple with only the core left. She was aware of standing on a platform of stone held up by an impossibly thin tendril of rock. Underfoot the ground seemed to shift and sway, dancing with the wind that blew against her body.

"My friends call me Nevada. But I guess you don't know me like that…"

Below, the world dropped away and didn't return for hundreds of feet, an impenetrable valley surrounded by knife points. Nevada didn't let herself look away. That would be admitting she was scared. And if she stopped moving—that was something a terrified woman would do.

"What do you want from me?" Nevada called, her voice echoing mockingly back from the surrounding karst.

The Lady's laughter was the same way, everywhere and nowhere, coming from Nevada's own head as much as anything else…

There! A face over Nevada's shoulder, in a blacked-out window of the hut. Jet black, only a few shades off from the shadows inside, but Nevada had made out a shape, an expression, a sense of life—horribly malignant life—like a part of this hateful landscape had been sculpted and brought to life, able to express the antipathy it had only been able to exist in before.

"You cannot imagine what I want," the Lady said. The voice sounded stronger ahead of her, so Nevada took another step and saw an opening in the hut, a door covered by a heavy curtain. "But what I need is to speak to you. To know you. We won't get another chance like this one. The next time we meet, things will be… difficult."

Nevada could smell burning herbs seeping out from inside. Imphepho. She forced herself not to cough. "If you want return customers that bad, maybe you could do something every five visits. Free drink. Maybe just validate parking, I don't know."

She pulled the curtain open, and despite shining right into the hut, the sunlight didn't seem to penetrate it. All Nevada could make out—as if she were standing in a dark room with only the moonlight to see by—was a table in the middle of the hut's one small room. On it was a deck of tarot cards.

"Come in. Sit. Sit. Do you know who I am?"

"Miss Cleo?" Nevada stepped inside. "I never did call you now for my free reading…"

When the curtain swept shut behind her, the darkness was absolute. Nevada froze, still aware of the abyss underneath her feet. She felt it keenly, as if one wrong step and those karst spikes would be rushing up to meet her. And as her eyes adjusted to the darkness, she became aware of the shadow on the other side of the table, a shape that hadn't been there before but was there *now*. Gaining more reality, more certainty in her mind as she breathed and waited and—

A match was struck. In the sudden light—a horribly inadequate light among miles of darkness—Nevada could see the woman. Ebony skin. White lipstick, handprints of white paint on her cheeks and throat. A tailcoat was buttoned over her breasts but opened to show her ribs, white tattoos showing where they lay below the skin. Small bones were tied in her dreadlocked hair, rattling away as she moved the match to a votive candle on the table. The light lingered after she waved the match out, but it was sickly, anemic. The darkness ate away at it like cancer took healthy cells.

"I am Lady Tendai," the woman said. "And you killed two of my men."

"Actually, there were these alligators," Nevada started. "Nah, fuck it. If you have something to say to me, say it."

"I have nothing to be said to you," Tendai demurred. "The cards. The cards wish to speak. They speak through me, knowing all, saying all, but you do not listen. I listen. I hear."

Nevada sat down across from her. "Just so you know, I ate Chinese the other night, so I've already had my fortune. I'm going to be really pissed if you guys can't agree with each other. Already bought a Lotto ticket."

"Your jokes can't hide you," Tendai said. "You think nothing serious can happen if you take nothing seriously. It makes me wonder—how long did it take you to joke about how pale your brother was as he bled out from the leg you cost him?"

Nevada smiled. "If I were you, I'd stop looking forward to that next run-in we're supposed to have. Shuffle the damn cards."

Tendai spread her arms in a long shrug. "I am *sungoma.* I cannot do magic for you unless you give me silver. Something personal."

"Geez, I knew that framed photo of Elvis would come in handy. Would you take an IOU?"

"The locket," Tendai said.

Nevada's hand jumped to her throat. The locket was nothing much. A hunk of silver and an old picture. The only baby picture she had. The only sight of her son she could stomach.

When this was all over, she'd get another one. She'd find out how he had grown up. Before she could stop herself, Nevada ripped the locket off and slapped it down onto the table. "Deal."

Tendai's spindly fingers crossed the table to pick up the locket. Her knuckles were tattooed as white as bone. She pulled the locket back, and without seeming to put it anywhere, began to shuffle the deck of cards. The tattoos of her fingers in motion were like the white gleam on a scorpion's shiny black carapace.

"I know who you are," Nevada said. "Some skank who thinks she's hot shit because she shacked up with yet another African warlord. My condolences on the drone strike. But just so you know, getting power because of who you married is so two-thousand-late. Didn't work for Hillary, won't work for you."

"My husband is the Baron Samedi," Tendai said. She shuffled with one hand as her right came up to brush over the white tattoos almost glowing on her dark flesh. "You see where he kisses me? Where he touches me? Death himself is my master."

"I don't have a master," Nevada retorted. "I'm what you'd call self-employed."

"You're alone," Tendai said. "But not always. Let us see where you have been and where you will go before Death claims you." She spread the cards across the table. "Draw three."

Nevada reached out at random, pulling three cards across to her end of the table. She didn't flip them over. "Speaking of the past, the present, and the future, why do you want the skulls? And what's Singh want with them?"

Tendai ran her fingers over the drawn cards without exactly touching them, without yet flipping them over. "Singh is a powerful man. When he sees something he can't control, he sees in it more power. And when he sees power, he wants that power for himself."

"Can he get it?"

"No. This is not possible." Tendai shook her head for emphasis. The bones rattled around her face. "He thinks he understands them, but he doesn't."

"You do?"

"I understand enough. But if you wish to understand the past..." Tendai gestured to the first of Nevada's cards before pulling her hands back, setting them in her lap.

Nevada flipped over the first card. The Empress, upside-down.

"Your past," Tendai said. "Motherhood, but reversed. What could that mean, I wonder?"

"Yeah, yeah, big mystery. Can we move on? I remember my past. I was there."

"Do you?" Tendai asked. "Do you let yourself remember? Have you told Candice about the child's father? Why you kept the baby?"

Nevada just looked at her. "Thin ice, Madame Zeroni. Thin fucking ice."

"I see why you are in such a hurry to get to the present. Go on, Thea. Turn the card over."

"How about no?" Nevada clapped her hand down on the card to hold it in place. "Tell me about the skulls. Who made them? What are they for?"

Tendai only laughed. "You make the same mistake Singh has made. You assume in your arrogance that you are smart enough to comprehend the ways of those who are outside all your understandings, other than everything you know. Beings who walk over our world as easily as we would step over an anthill."

"Aliens?" Nevada scoffed. "You're telling me I've been picking up ET's lunchboxes all this time?"

Tendai brought up her hands and spread them apart. "Today, they are called aliens. Yesterday, they were fairies and angels. Who knows what they'll be called tomorrow? Turn over the next card. Let us see what the cards have in store for you today."

Almost growling, Nevada twisted the card face-up. A naked man and a naked woman. The Lovers. "Hunh," she said. "So, me and Candice—which one of us is the guy?"

"The cards can be blunt sometimes. Shall we see what the future will bring?"

Nevada put her pointer finger on the future card, then used her middle finger to spin it around, whirling it one way, then the other. "Say I believe you. Say aliens made the skulls. Why? What do they do?"

Tendai craned her head back and laughed, a single war whoop of a chuckle. "Do? Why should they do anything? Still the same arrogance, still thinking everything is a toy you can play with. But you're right in one respect. Even among the gods, there are accidents. A ship sinks. A car breaks down. A forest burns. Things that are not meant for this world come to us."

Nevada huffed a laugh, her shoulders shaking. "That's it, then? It really is ET's lunchbox, after all that."

"Or a father's gun, found by a child." Tendai pointed her forefinger at Nevada, her thumb sticking up, her other fingers curled into a fist. "Bang."

"I'd prefer a nine-millimeter. More ergonomic." Nevada flipped over the last card. Death. She wasn't surprised.

"There you have it," Tendai said apologetically. "Your present may be love, but I fear someone you love will not survive. I'm sorry, Thea. The cards have had their say."

"You know what I say?" Before Tendai could react, Nevada's hand lashed out and grabbed the deck of cards. "I say I've had enough of your Penn and Teller *bullshit*."

She threw the cards up in the air. They came back down, crashing all over the tabletop, and on each one, the picture was of her son.

Nevada leapt up, staggering away from the table, losing sight of Tendai in the encroaching darkness. She kicked out with a foot—caught the table, turning it over, the candle going flying but not finding Tendai with any of the light it shed. The hut was empty. There was only darkness.

Nevada backed up, felt the curtain behind her, and as soon as she did, she threw it open and rushed out. Her boots knocked grit off the edge of the stone, out into space, and she drove herself around the hut until she collapsed against the post holding the bridge up. Butch was there at the other end. The Zuni and the bandaged man, to her utter lack of surprise, were gone.

"Easy?" Butch called across the gap. "You okay? What happened?"

Nevada struggled to catch her breath. "We played cards. I got a bad hand. You?"

Butch held up the tablet. "The *Liparus*. It's an oil tanker. And Singh is very keen that nobody knows about it."

Nevada started across the bridge, heedless of whether it would support her or not. If it had the balls to break on her, she'd burn it the fuck down. "Where is it?"

"Off the coast of Somalia. *The Blue Lagoon* can make it in five days if I push it, four if we're lucky."

Nevada punched his arm as she reached him. "Then why are we standing around jabbering? Fuck Tendai. Let's go."

Butch turned to follow her with his eyes as she marched past him. "Tendai? Like the Spider-Man chick?"

"I don't want to talk about that shit."

"No wonder." Butch trailed after her. "They're nowhere near as good as the Andrew Garfield movies were..."

CHAPTER 13

Candice had another busy day lined up. Her room was longer than it was wide. She could walk nine paces before having to turn around and walk the other way. She'd do that until breakfast was served, then until lunch, then until supper, with breaks for bathroom visits. At least the toilet was in her quarters. Then again, walking to a second location would be a nice change of pace.

Change of pace. Funny. Nine steps. Turn around, go again.

At one point, she'd catalogued how many steps she took in a day, between breakfast and lunch, between lunch and supper, but the facts had left her mind. Probably self-sabotage. Too depressing to have those numbers in her head. How long did she have to memorize them? A year? Two years? How much could she take before she went mad?

Nine steps. Turn around, go again.

She'd written an entire franchise of horror movies on things she'd like to see happen to Singh and Gore. Did it count as going mad for her to script two hours of bad things happening to eyeballs, then write a teeth-themed sequel? Maybe. But the alternative was thinking of suicide, and she couldn't think about that.

She wouldn't have to think too hard, after all. How difficult could it be to get herself killed when every one of Gore's men carried rifles on their shoulder? But she couldn't do that. Nevada was out there, making her way to her, and if nothing else, Candice wanted to see what she did to Singh and Gore when she got here.

Nine steps. Turn around, go again.

What five days of isolation really did was give her time to ask the one question she didn't want answered. After all this time, why was she still so certain that Nevada would come for her? It was an unshakable faith she didn't want to go away, but at the same time, a part of her couldn't let it go unexamined. How did she know Nevada wasn't dead, given up on her, or just would never find her?

The only answer she could hit, as her head spun around in the same circles her body was going in, was that she would do the same for Nevada if their situations were reversed.

The hatch moaned as it opened. Candice started. Breakfast already? Usually it wasn't for another twenty minutes. Was she losing track of time now? She didn't know whether the thought comforted her or not. Imagine thinking only weeks had passed, then finding she was forty years older.

Guns poked through the open hatch, aimed at her. Candice madly thought of rushing them, knowing they would take her life. But Nevada was somewhere out there. Looking for her. Caring if she lived or died.

She went quietly.

Gore stared at the Bell 212 helicopter hanging in the air, fifty feet up from the deck of the *Liparus*, the two tons of machinery it was delivering hanging from a high-tension cable. He felt the 212's wake as it hovered lower, threading the needle of its payload into the door to the *Liparus*'s cargo hold.

The tachyon emitter would soon be in place, and this shitshow would be over. Still, even though the finish line was in sight, he kept an eye on the 212. If the pilot lost control, Gore would have to make sure Singh was out of the way when it crashed. Man couldn't sign a check if he was dead.

Singh breathed in the sea air—clotted by diesel fumes as it was—and let out a satisfied exhale. "How does it feel, Mr. Gore? We're on the next stage of human advancement. 'Course, I'm used to glory. I don't think I've ever been in a building that's less than twenty stories, but you—this must be an entirely new experience for you. You're stepping into a history book."

"Thought I stepped in something," Gore muttered.

He briefly took his eyes off the 212 and scanned the horizon. There was almost nothing; the endless shifting of waves and clouds had long since made him lose all orientation to the nearest land. But the speck he'd noticed on the horizon that morning was now a scale model. Gore drew a spotting scope from his pocket.

“That fishing boat is still here,” he said, looking through it.

“Fishing takes a long time?” Singh replied, putting a lot of effort into sounding shocked. “Who knew?”

“We should terminate them. Just to be safe.”

Candice appeared on the deck, shoved along by the two guards escorting her. She blinked and twisted her head away from the cold light of day. Gore tried to think of how many days she’d been under artificial lights. Five? Had it been that long already?

“Why? To them, we’re just an oil tanker having a part delivered.” Singh patted Gore on the back. “If they see something, we can always kill them then. But until that time, it seems to me we should appreciate the value of human life.”

Singh clapped his hands as Candice reached them, trudging up the stairs to their vantage point on a catwalk. The guards stayed at the bottom of the steps.

“Candice! Good, good! So glad you were able to find an opening in your schedule.” He tittered. “He—” Singh glanced at Gore, then looked away just as quickly. “Well, some people, they can’t appreciate what we’re doing. I thought you might. You deserve to see the fruits of your labor; this is all thanks to you. And don’t think I don’t appreciate it.”

Candice said nothing.

“Do you like the outfit?” Singh spread his arms. He wore a blue silk *sherwani* down to his knees, a white *churidar* on his legs, and *mojari* shoes that curled at the tip. A golden turban was tied around his head. Pearls were studded all through the ensemble, set at his wrists, his collar, and across his turban like a crown. “I always dress for the occasion.”

“What do you want, Singh?” Candice asked flatly.

“How about a civil tone to start with? You know, you’ve had free room and board for the past week, I haven’t asked you to help out any, you haven’t had to do any chores. There are people sleeping in cardboard boxes —”

“Sir,” Gore interrupted, bringing Singh’s attention to the helicopter.

Inside the hold, workers had detached the cable from the crate. The 212 reeled its cable in, turning to depart. Gore signaled it to move off, and the 212 lowered its nose, angling into a course away from the *Liparus*.

"Come on, come on!" Singh cried, leading the way to the elevator. Candice trailed after him, Gore behind to ensure she didn't wander off. "You won't want to miss this."

Two miles away, Butch stood on the deck of the *Blue Lagoon*, staring at the oil tanker through a set of field binoculars. He was shirtless, which revealed the diamond shape tattooed on his upper arm, four more rhombuses divided inside it, forming an X. Jean cut-offs and hemp sandals were the only other coverings on his body.

"I have eyes on the target," he said, lowering the binos. "Hey, can I just say, 'I'm looking at the target'? I've been saying 'eyes on the target' for a while, but now everyone's doing it and it's not cool no more."

Out of sight in the boat's crew quarters, Nevada zipped up her wetsuit. "You can do whatever you want, Butch. We're not actually in the military."

"I don't know—KISS Army," Butch muttered. "Hey, just because Singh is there, you sure Candice is?"

"For his sake, he'd better hope so." Nevada poked her head out of the hold. "Lose the binoculars. They see you looking at them with those, they're going to shoot you."

"You're always saying they're going to shoot me. How many times have people shot me?"

"Four," Nevada replied.

"Well, that's not going to happen this time. I have the perfect cover." He picked up a shirt from the handrail and slipped it on. The graphic on the front read *Women Want Me, Fish Fear Me*. "I'm just a salty sea dog riding the waves and catching some fish."

"What about the harpoon gun?" Nevada asked, nodding to the boat's prow.

"Big fish," Butch reasoned. "You wanna move on to the equipment check?"

"Let's move on," Nevada agreed.

Butch had laid out her equipment on a table in the hold, along with the dry bag it would go into. He looked over each item before putting it in the bag. "SIG P210, assorted ammo. I'm expecting this back, but then I was expecting the other two back also."

He tossed them in, then picked up a bullpup assault rifle and several box magazines. "Steyr AUG, carbon fiber stock, Corvus Defensio rail with laser sight. Suppressor's on, so you won't have to learn sign language anytime soon. Lightweight plastic, shouldn't give you any trouble handling it."

It went into the bag. Next, a stack of black bricks the size of a deck of playing cards. With them was a yellow remote unit—all of it wrapping paper for a red button with a plastic cover over it.

"Thermite charges, remote detonator. Arm the charge like so—" Butch slid a tab over on one of the bricks. "Detonates once it gets the signal."

Nevada took the charge from him and slid the tab back. "I don't know, seems hard to remember. Maybe if the instructions rhymed?"

Butch held open the bag for her to drop it in. "Be careful with that. The government doesn't want you to know this, but that kind of ordnance brought down the World Trade Center."

"It did not," Nevada said.

Butch stuffed the rest of the charges into the bag. "I have some documentaries that I think will make you see things differently. We can watch those after. They're long because they're thorough."

Nevada snapped her fingers. "Get killed and don't come back, got it. What else?"

Butch picked up a puck the size of a casino chip. "Wi-Fi camera blocker. Adhesive strip on the back, just peel off the Band-Aid thing. You put this within three feet of a camera, it hacks the signal and loops the footage." A USB drive. "Rootkit hack. Plug this into an alarm, it disables the entire system. No sirens, no flashing lights; you push the button as many times as you want, nothing." A bulletproof vest. "Bulletproof vest. Helpful tip: it only protects the part of your body that it's covering, so try not to get shot anywhere else." Brass knuckles, only with a thick plate on the business end. "Magnetic clamps." He picked one up like a steam iron. "Thumb goes here. You throw the switch, magnet turns on, you pull yourself. Switch off, magnet off, you can wave it around, do what you want with it, I don't care." A ring as big as the circle a man's thumb and forefinger made. "Safecracker. Put this on a combination lock, it spins the dial around, listens for the little—you know what, you probably won't need that, forget it." He took the ring off the table. "Yeah, magnetic clamp. I think that's the last thing; that's everything."

"Are you sure?" Nevada asked. "Are you sure that's everything?"

"Oh, right." Butch reached out, putting a big hand on her shoulder. "You've got this, Sis. I believe in you."

"No, it was a legitimate question. Is that absolutely everything?"

"Yeah, what else would you need?"

"I don't know. I'm asking you."

"Well, I can't think of anything else."

Nevada groaned. "We can't act like this when Candice gets here. You're going to embarrass me."

"Okay, from here on out, we make a list, we write everything down. That way we'll be sure."

"That's good. Write that down."

"You have a pen?"

Nevada looked at the table before she could stop herself. "I'm just gonna go."

Butch nodded. "Yeah, you don't want to overthink this."

"I don't think that'll be a problem." Nevada looked over at the weapons rack—all the hardware she couldn't take with her unless she wanted to give herself a cardiac arrest on the way. "What about the M82a1?"

"The antimaterial rifle?" Butch asked. "That's mine. I don't think you can even lift it. It's metal."

"Yeah, yeah, don't shoot your toe off with it. Lots of girls have foot fetishes these days and you need all the help you can get."

Nevada checked her scuba gear one last time, the oxygen regulator hanging at her breastbone, the goggles strapped to her forehead. "Funny how you think you'll have time to say every little thing. Then you run out."

"What do we have to talk about?" Butch asked, arms crossing. "We grew up together. Two decades under the same roof. What's left to say? You borrowed my favorite Hot Wheels and never gave it back?"

"I'm sorry." Nevada swallowed. She'd never been more aware of how her words started in her chest, swelled in her throat, then surged out of her mouth. "I read somewhere that most cases of postpartum depression—they're because women don't bond with their kids right away. It takes a while. I didn't have that. I was in love with my baby first time I saw him. And I gave him away. I lost him. Can't forget what that felt like. When you got hurt, it all came back. I left you and I knew you'd hate me, you'd hate the sight of me, but I'd know you were okay. I guess I knew I could live with that."

"I don't hate you," Butch said.

Nevada stood there.

Butch cleared his throat. "Well, good luck."

"You really don't want to elaborate *any* on that?"

"God, you're needy." Butch set his hands on her upper arms. "You're my sister. I love you. And I had kinda already figured out you were a bitch."

"Okay. Cool. I'm gonna expect a gift at Christmas."

"I actually celebrate the winter solstice now."

Nevada blinked and held her eyes shut for a long time before opening them again. "Have fun with the fishing."

"Have fun storming the oil tanker."

Nevada gave herself a moment of tension—squeezing her fists into perfect circles—then she released her breath. It felt like she had a million things to do: Jacques, her son, a laundry list of instructions she should make in case she didn't make it back. But she couldn't let them have any hold on her. She was coming back, with Candice. She wouldn't imagine anything else, wouldn't let it get any more of a foothold on her reality.

Pulling her dive mask over her eyes and slotting the mouthpiece between her teeth, Nevada ran up the stairs and slipped over the side. She dropped into the water with a splash that was only there for a split second.

As it operated, the tachyon emitter didn't spin around or light up or have any ostentatious special effects. It only let out a series of stuttering clicks. When it was done, though, the skull that had been placed in its chamber seemed to catch the light more. To Candice, it felt more menacing somehow. Like there was something inside the translucent contours, small but virulent, a wasp buzzing around looking for a way out of its jar.

A man in a hazmat suit took the skull away. Another was in the isolation chamber, holding the next skull to be charged while the airlock cycled. The tachyon emitter rested, a low hum tingling around it. Status bars climbed as it accepted the new power being fed into it.

It was usually easy for Candice not to talk, especially when she was nervous. But now she was so nervous that words were spinning within her, around and around and around. She had to let them out before they flew right off the track.

"I think I know what they are," she said.

Gore ignored her, smoking a cigarette with fingers dripping darkness. As a long drag annihilated the tip of the cigarette, leaving only ash, he plucked the spent portion from the end and rubbed it between his fingers, mixing the exhausted tobacco with his blackened sweat.

Candice pressed on. "Something Nevada said. You were listening, right? One-legged man to an ass-kicking contest. And he said one of them was metal. What if that's all they are? The skulls? Metal legs."

"It doesn't matter what they are," Singh said, sounding far away. He bounced on his heels. "How long until the machine's ready again?"

"Two minutes, forty-three seconds," Gore said.

"You didn't even check your watch..."

Candice felt like she was bursting open. "What if they're prosthetics? Not for us, obviously, but for—something else. You've heard about the Singularity, right? Man and machine becoming one, people uploading, digitizing their minds? What if that's what it looks like for them? Their brain, their mind..." She gestured frantically. "Whatever body they had is long gone, but the consciousness remains. In those. They're escape pods. Lifeboats. Preserving their memories and their thoughts until—"

Singh looked at her. His eyes—they seemed to catch the light too. "Until they're rescued."

Candice nodded. "Until they send out a distress signal."

Singh shrugged. "It doesn't really matter one way or the other. All that matters is that they send out a beacon and something answers."

The tachyon emitter's hum rose to a fever pitch. The next skull was placed inside it.

"Oh God," Candice muttered. "First contact with an alien race and we're being represented by—you."

Singh actually looked hurt for a moment. "Rude. Don't worry yourself, Cushing. We won't be saying anything to them."

Gore dropped his cigarette to the floor of the hold and quickly lit another. The machine's hum became a single shrill note, then deafening silence, relieved only by click after click. Like the lock on a safe was being turned.

Nevada kicked through the hazy blue of the sea, making a machine of herself: deep and even breaths, pumping legs, arms held sleekly to her sides. She favored her arms as much as possible on the swim. She'd need upper-body strength to make the climb, so for now, it was leg day.

Visibility was next to nothing—shades of darkening blue collapsing in on each other within a few yards. She looked up. Above the surface of the water, she could at least make out the towering superstructure of the tanker, rising up from the ship's stern to loom over the hold that took up much of the hull. The accommodation area. The bridge.

That would be her target. If she climbed up onto the deck, it'd be too easy for them to pin her down and flush her out at their leisure. In the claustrophobically close quarters of the superstructure, its corridors and crew rooms, she'd have maneuverability on her side. A scalpel cutting wherever it wanted on a vast, unwieldy body.

Having oriented herself, Nevada looked back down in time to see the seventeen feet of great white shark in front of her. She stopped kicking. The shark spent a moment as a distant shadow, then came fully into view, lazy twists of its dorsal fin propelling it forward. Ribbons of sunlight came through the waves overhead and rippled on its gray hide.

Nevada took a deep breath, hearing the air hissing through her scuba tank—she kicked again. The shark's black eyes regarded her as they passed, ships in the night. Nevada resolved to make herself a machine again. Steady, careful pumps of her legs. She could see other shapes in the distance; more sharks or their prey, she couldn't tell. All she could do was tell herself that either the great white would bite her or it wouldn't. Nothing else had changed.

The rudder of the tanker and its motionless props swam into view. Nevada caught sight of a shark—either the same one as before or a new one—out of the corner of her eye. She ignored it, keeping to the same unhurried pace as the tanker came up to embrace her.

She stopped kicking, spun herself upright, and reached out with her flippers to stop herself. The barnacle-encrusted hull was nothing she wanted to touch bare-handed. The British Navy used to torture people that way.

Two clamps hung from a lanyard around her neck. She took them in hand, kicked up to the surface, and breached. She pressed the clamp in her right hand to the hull and thumbed the switch. It clanged resoundingly as magnetism pulled it firmly against the metal hull.

Pulling herself up with that handhold, Nevada set the clamp in her left hand a few feet higher, then thumbed that switch too. Another sonorous clang. She disengaged the first clamp, reached up with it, turned it back on, and pulled herself fully out of the water. Only then did she look back over her shoulder.

She could easily count at least twenty fins carving out circles in the deep blue sea.

"Cool," Nevada said, and kept climbing.

A guard stood outside the superstructure of the *Liparus* on an exterior stairwell that ran up from the deck to the bridge, smoking, relaxing, until his cigarette was just a butt. He tried to get one last drag out of it, then tossed it over the side.

A moment later, it flew back, landing at his feet. He stooped to examine it before he thought to look where it had come from and turned in time to see Nevada fling herself over the railing. She drove his head into the wall.

Nevada had stripped off her flippers, air tank, goggles, and the top half of her scuba suit. It hung down from her waist, leaving her bare except for a bikini top and the bulletproof vest she'd put on over that. Picking through the dry bag, Nevada slotted ammo for her sidearm and AUG into loops of fabric sewn into the vest. She'd already strapped a holster for the P210 to her thigh and slung the AUG over her shoulder. The magnetic clamps hung around her neck again.

"Hey there," Nevada said to the semiconscious man. She aimed the P210 at him. "Welcome back. Let's try to keep it down, huh? People have work in the morning."

"What do you want?" the guard asked her.

With her free hand, Nevada reached into her opened dry bag, picked out a box magazine for the AUG, and fixed it into her vest. "Where's the girl?"

"What girl?"

"How many girls are you holding hostage on this boat? Candice Cushing. Tall, black, blonde hair, enough curves for a go-kart track. If you have more than one like that, I suppose I'll take both…"

The guard grimaced at her. "If you shoot me, they'll hear it for miles."

"Oh yeah?" Nevada extended the pistol closer to him. "What do you care? You'll be dead. And if you're not going to talk, then you don't need a throat—"

He swallowed, giving a minute shake of his head. "You can't win. Gore will see you coming a mile away."

Sighing, Nevada struck him across the temple with the butt of her P210. He slumped to the ground like it was a waterbed. "Gore is never even going to know I was here."

The hatch to the superstructure's interior swung open, the guard already speaking as he came out. "Foster, break's over, stub it out and—"

He saw Nevada. He went for his gun. By then, Nevada had already put four holes in his chest.

The tachyon emitter stopped clicking. Silence reigned. The sixth skull was taken away. The seventh was brought out of the isolation chamber.

When the machine started humming again, there was an added resonance, an echo that hadn't been there before. Candice saw the others stiffen too. Whatever the skulls were doing, it was happening faster now. Happening more.

An alarm went off, klaxons shrieking off the walls in distended harmony, echoes turning the noise into Theremin music.

"Shut that off!" Singh shouted. Candice had never heard him so loud. Offended. *Incensed.*

Gore was already barking into his walkie-talkie. "Kill it! Kill the alarm. Someone *tell me* what's going on…"

He broke off, seeing the smile on Candice's face, the stare that coolly bore into him when he looked at her.

"What are you looking at?"

"Probably where the first bullet's going to go."

Gore shook his head. "She's not here, Cushing. She's not coming. There isn't even a—"

The alarm cut off, leaving behind a dwindling sound like wobbling sheet metal, as if to make room for the realization hitting Gore.

He brought the walkie-talkie to his mouth and barked at it like a dog behind a fence. "I want a launch going out in sixty seconds, four-man fire team. Go to the fishing boat, kill everything onboard. If a seagull lands on the railing, shoot it."

His words didn't shake Candice's confidence. She kept staring, wondering if his flop sweat would be black too.

Gore reached out to grasp Singh's shoulder. The blackness on his fingers instantly soaked into Singh's *sherwani*. "Sir, we might want to think about preparing for launch."

Singh turned his head to take Gore in. It seemed difficult—like gears inside him had rusted. "Already? Yes, yes, whatever you think is best…"

Gore offered Candice a smile. It wasn't black; it just seemed that way somehow. "It can't be stopped now. It's happening. Nothing changes that."

"Let me know when you're done writing the history book," Candice said.

Gore brought his walkie-talkie up again. His finger traced over the push-to-talk button while calm flooded his features. Then, holding it down, he spoke softly. "Open it up."

More echoes danced through the hold, but now they seemed somehow to precede the noise that should've caused them. It took Candice a moment to realize what was happening. Some gigantic mechanism was hurtling into motion, gears rolling, chains pulling. The far end of the hold was *spreading*—the bow of the ship actually opening at the top, high above the waterline, letting in a flood of sunlight. Candice shielded her eyes. Like some huge, saurian set of jaws, the hold of the *Liparus* was now open to the world.

"Four to go," Singh muttered, looking on as the eighth skull was taken from the isolation chamber.

Pressed against the inside of a corner in the endless series of corridors and hatches that made up the accommodation area of the tanker, Nevada drew her dive knife. She held it out past the corner, seeing the surveillance camera watching this section of hallway in the blade's reflection. Quickly sheathing it again, she took out one of Butch's camera blockers and peeled off the backing. Judging that there were about three feet between where she was and the camera, she reached up to stick the blocker against the uppermost part of the wall.

The adhesive clung onto the wall for only a second before the whole thing slipped off.

"C'mon, Butch," Nevada muttered before taking her AUG and smashing in the camera with the rifle butt.

"Hey!" A man leaned out of one of the rooms along the hall, the strap of a rifle cutting across his chest. "What are you doing?"

Nevada flashed him her best smile and walked up to him like she wasn't carrying two thousand dollars worth of military hardware in her hands. "I know it looks weird, but it's actually really technical. You see, I take the butt of the rifle—"

Closing to arm's reach, she swung the AUG's stock across his face, hard enough to hockey-puck his nose into the next county. He went down to his knees, but she heard a muttered curse behind her—a quick glance showed her a crewman in the opposing room going for the gun at his hip. Nevada fired without aiming, a three-shot burst that threw him against the wall behind him and left most of his innards there.

The man she'd given a buttstroke to groaned, coming back to his feet. She elbowed a concussion into his skull, and he dropped for good. Nevada poked her head out into the corridor to see if anyone had heard.

A round thudded into her chest, slapping into the bulletproof vest she wore. Stinging pain filtered through to her breast, somewhere between being branded and throwing herself in front of a golf swing. Nevada jerked herself back, figured the last thing the oncoming goon squad would expect was for her to come right back out of cover, and slid out with her AUG at the ready.

She fired, swiveled, fired, swiveled, the laser sight scything from one target to another as she gave each man in the group a quick burst, bullets racing their reaction time. By the time the fourth man realized she was shooting the guy in front, three bullets were already on their way to his chest.

7.62mm rounds drilled into the doorway beside Nevada's head, angry hornets coming from the other end of the corridor. She threw herself back inside, nearly tripping over the henchman she'd concussed.

She kicked him over onto his back. He wasn't carrying any grenades. She yanked the Smith & Wesson Model 4006 from his holster, held her hand outside the door, and emptied the clip in the direction the shots had come from. Nevada had never had much use for .40 S&W anyway.

Dropping the sidearm, she unsheathed her knife and checked the reflection outside. Her blind fire had taken out the point man, maybe hobbled someone else, but that left three warm bodies. And from the other end of the corridor, she had another fire team incoming. A rock and a hard place, making an Easy Nevada sandwich.

Nevada looked around the room, evidently the quarters of the guy who had gotten all the enjoyment he ever would out of an intact skull. Nicer than her last apartment. Even had a view—a porthole looking out at the ocean.

"Hey, guys, are you looking for an intruder-type person?" she called. "Because I think I saw one in the mess hall. I'd check it out if I were you."

"You're gonna die, bitch!"

"That's uncalled for. I was just trying to help." Nevada reached behind herself, taking a thermite charge from its holder at the small of her back. She planted it against the hatch. Like modelling clay, the explosive inside the open-ended plastic holder clung where she pressed it. "Hey, long as we're shooting the breeze, who do you think killed all the dead guys out there? Because I have no idea."

"You're dead!"

"Eat shit and die, asshole!" Nevada retorted. She did an active reload, taking out the half-empty clip from her AUG, trading it for a fresh magazine, and saving the leftovers for later. "See, now we're a YouTube comment section. Are you happy?"

"Fuck you!"

Nevada rolled her eyes. "Why do I even bother?"

She drew her P210 and poked her arm out to fire a few quick shots in both directions. Three seconds later, she pulled her hand back, but not before return fire traced a furrow across her elbow. Nevada winced and translated it into motion, throwing herself to the other end of the quarters and knocking out the glass of the porthole. Hopefully the ringing in everyone's ears would drown out the noise.

She cleared the glass away as much as possible with the barrel of the AUG, then unclipped the clamps from her lanyard. Reaching out through the porthole, she set them on either side and thumbed the magnets on. Then, biting back several cliché lines about weight loss, she pulled herself outside, transferring her weight first to one clamp, then both of them.

Halfway through the porthole, she froze dead. The sky was the same, the horizon was the same, but the sea—the waves weren't going in the right direction. They overlapped, crossing each other, half going one way, half going the opposite way, their swells forming a grid. It looked *wrong*. Unnatural. And the grid was lifting itself up, growing more extreme, like a seismograph registering bigger and bigger tremors.

"Move in, move in!" she heard behind her, the usual sparkling repartee. Nevada quickly hauled herself the rest of the way out.

Now hanging outside the porthole, bridged between the two clamps, she thumped the magnet off in the left one and stretched down with it as far as she could before she triggered it again. Then Nevada turned off the clamp in her right hand and let herself drop down to catch herself on her left hand's grip. Repeated the process with her left hand, then again, dropping down the ship's hull in sharp jerks, each time feeling like she was making headway on popping a shoulder out of its socket.

She heard the gunmen tromping through the room she'd vacated, overturning furniture, searching for her. It would be bare seconds until they looked out the porthole. Nevada let go with her left hand and reached into a pocket on her vest. She dug into it until her hand closed around the remote detonator…

"She's here!" The voice was above her; she had a heartbeat before he brought his gun to bear.

Nevada flicked the safety cover off the detonator. "Just no talking to some people."

The *Liparus* shook. Gore swayed in automatic counterbalance to the tremor, while Singh fell to one knee. Candice saw confusion rippling through the assembled gunmen and workers and drank it in like mother's milk.

"That sounded close," she quipped.

"Shut up!" Singh lunged to his feet. "Shut up!"

He grabbed for the pistol in Gore's holster, but Gore seized his wrist, refusing to let him draw the gun.

"I think this is one insurance policy we should let pay out, don't you?" Gore asked.

He shook Singh's hand loose; Singh withdrew it without the pistol.

"I want us in position," Singh said. "I want to be ready to launch now."

Gore glanced at the isolation chamber, taking his walkie-talkie in hand. The tenth skull was being brought out of the cycling airlock. He spoke into the walkie-talkie. "Patch me into the PA system."

"I said now!" Singh insisted, voice raised.

"Bring it up," Gore called. With a shrug, he removed a slim tablet from the inside of his jacket. He showed the screen to Singh. "Very simple interface. Guidance system does all the work."

Candice heard squealing—tires—and turned to see something coming down the track that had been laid on the floor, moving into position at the open bow of the *Liparus*. A motorized sled, forty feet long, crawled along the track. On it was something Candice could barely recognize from grainy CNN footage. Six tons. A fuselage almost as long as a metro bus. A SCUD missile, with struts underneath it extending up, raising the missile into position.

Gore was still talking. "Once the target's locked in, green button starts the launch cycle, red button aborts the launch. There's another interface on the launcher itself, same system, but you don't want to be in the blast radius when the countdown finishes." He shook the tablet. "Safer just to use this."

"Our first contact with an alien civilization and you brought a missile?" Candice demanded.

"No," Gore said. "We brought two. Always have a spare." He spoke into the walkie-talkie again. "How's it coming with the PA system?"

Below deck, Nevada followed the grinding heartbeat of the ship's engine until she came to its source. The engine room was a vast sprawl of diesel machinery and DOS computers, pipes and pumps and grease, with several crewmen working over it like ants at a picnic. For a moment, no one noticed her. Not seeing any guns, Nevada marched right in and raised her voice.

"Everybody! Everybody, could I have your attention, please? I'm going to need everyone to line up in an orderly fashion and calmly proceed to the lifeboats."

All of the crewmen eyed her with confusion, but only one of them spoke up. "What's the emergency?"

Nevada unslung her AUG. "Me," she said, and fired a burst into the ceiling.

The evacuation wasn't very orderly, but she couldn't fault them for speed. Looking over the main engine, the diesel generators, the bilge pumps, Nevada found a recess underneath some machinery—the entrance to a crawlspace accommodating some pipes. One by one, she took out her thermite charges, armed them, and pitched them into the crawlspace. She was about to throw the last one when she heard the PA system boom.

"Ms. Nevada." Gore's voice. "Ms. Easy Nevada—I assume that's you, because everyone else who's had the misfortune to stand in our way is currently dead. To go out on a still-further limb, let us assume you're here for Cushing. I have her here; I'm looking at her now. Down the sights of my gun."

Candice's voice. "Easy, don't—"

Her words died as quickly as they'd started up. Nevada felt a pang like she'd swallowed something sharp. She had to remind herself not to tighten her fist too much or she'd crush the thermite charge in her hand.

"If you *do* want her, she's here in the hold with fifty of my best men. If you come here and surrender yourself in the next five minutes, she lives. Or you can listen to her die while we hunt you down and kill you anyway. I leave the choice with you."

Nevada heard herself snarl. She forced nonchalance, tossing the last thermite charge up in the air and catching it.

"Shouldn't have told me where you were, asshole. Hiding was your best bet."

CHAPTER 14

The twelfth skull was placed into the tachyon emitter. Gore now watched it the same way Singh did—like a gambler at a horse race watching his bet be overtaken as it came to the finish line.

Candice supposed it wasn't too moral to take this much satisfaction in their panic, but then, she was an archaeologist. She was trained to have an appreciation for dead people.

"Any special requests for your funerals?" she asked. "Cremation? Burial at sea? I have to think both are equally likely at this point..."

Gore whirled on her with a rage Singh could never be capable of. It burned in his eyes like something radioactive, something long ago contaminated. "I wouldn't be so smug if I were you. Your friend's always been much better at ending lives than saving them. That's why we hired her."

"I'm not the one she wants to end."

Gore ran his hands over his face, streaking black sweat across his features, and it looked more like he was clawing something off of his face than painting something on. "Fuck this," he said, grabbing Candice by the hair and forcing her to come with him as he marched for the isolation chamber.

"Where are you going?" Singh demanded, struggling to keep up.

"Some added insurance. We built the isolation chamber to be a bank vault you can see through. Cushing's inside it, Nevada can't get to her. She tries anything, I shoot the girl; she can't stop me."

He bodily threw Candice into the airlock. Her stoicism came to a stop. "'The girl'? I have a name."

"You have one minute," Gore said, stepping into the airlock and pounding the button to cycle it into the isolation chamber.

"What about me?" Singh asked. He stood there as the airlock's outer door closed in front of him.

"You're safer out there," Gore insisted. "If Nevada does anything to you, I kill her gal pal."

"Okay," Singh said uncertainly. "Wait, what if I was in there with Cushing and *you*—"

The stern end of the hold exploded, the blast punching out of the pump room on the other side of the wall, smashing through the double hull and breaching into the hold. The sound was monstrous, echoing off the metal walls like the roar of a behemoth, doubling men over, making them drop their weapons and cover their ears.

The fireball rolled sideways, scorching metal for yards and yards before its appetite was appeased. Then it flickered out, leaving a haze of smoke, all the better to trap the shaft of light plunging into the hold, into the shadows where even the open bow's sunlight didn't reach.

The roar died down, leaving behind footsteps. Easy Nevada stepped into the opening she'd blasted through the wall, the light from behind her punching her silhouette into the hold.

"Hey, you with the bad hair!"

Fifty guns came up, slides racked, rounds chambered.

"You all looked."

Fifty bullets flew, and fifty more, and fifty more—

Nevada ducked back inside the pump room, taking cover as the barrage flew into the room. Most of it hit the pump directly opposite the opening, a monolithic thing the size of a Volkswagen, designed to keep crude oil flowing through a sixteen-inch hose at the speed of commerce. Ricochets bounced off it and clattered through the room, an indoor hailstorm, a beehive where the swarm was made of lead. The pump cracked and dented and deformed with hundreds of bullets chiseling away at it, making Nevada think of a block of marble being carved by a sculptor in fast-forward. But the only thing left behind when the gunfire stopped was modern art.

"You missed!" she shouted once the last shell casing had fallen.

The PA system coughed. One of the ricochets had hit the nearest loudspeaker. Gore's voice came out like he had something in his throat. "My men are already on their way to box you in from the other side, Nevada. You've accomplished nothing."

"I got your attention!" Nevada poked her hand out into the open, the remote detonator in it. "You're a military man, Gore. You see this? Look a little familiar?"

She stepped out into the opening. Guns racked again, reloaded, but Gore cried out louder: "Hold your fire, hold your fire!"

Nevada took in the football fields of empty space, the men behind ballistic shields, MP5s aimed out at her. Singh. The isolation chamber. Gore and Candice inside it.

She walked into the hold. "Now, I'm not a real nautical type—don't know starboard from port—but it occurs to me that if someone got irresponsible and set off five thermite charges, like the one I just detonated in y'all's engine room… Well. Definitely have a hull breach on your hands. The fuel tank would probably go up. This boat wouldn't go anywhere anytime soon, assuming it doesn't sink, which would be my bet. I don't know, seems inconvenient. Probably get really awkward if whoever the fuck has a coast guard out here has to come out, haul your ass to shore, and ask what you're up to. But don't listen to me—you probably have a Plan B for that, right?"

Inside the isolation chamber, Candice made a move toward Nevada, but Gore hauled her back, shoved her to her knees. He snarled something into his walkie-talkie. Nevada kept moving forward, her hand held high, displaying the detonator like some religious icon demanding respect. And gunman after gunman backed out of the way as she came by.

"I'm probably dating myself here," Nevada continued, "but this seems like a good time for a Titanic crack. Which one do you want: 'I'll never let go, Jack'? 'My heart will go on'? 'Titanic was called the ship of dreams'—now that's a dark horse. Show of hands? Guys?" Nevada paused, examining the SCUD missile as she came up to it. "Hey, dudes—and appreciate that I don't say this often—what's with the rocket?"

Singh was short enough that he didn't need to cower behind the two bodyguards holding ballistic shields in front of him. He just had to huddle some. "You can't begin to understand what's happening here. You can't even grasp the slightest inkling—"

"Probably Russian, right?" Nevada interrupted, looking over the missile as she walked by it. "Fall of the Soviet Union and all that? Plus there's a big red star on it. Still, what are ya gonna do with it? Is it just, like, a conversation piece?"

"It's for the aliens!" Singh shouted.

Nevada stopped in her tracks. "Wow. And I thought the border wall was an overreaction." She started walking again.

"Not those—!" Singh sounded like he would be jumping up and down if that wouldn't take him out from behind cover. "The skulls! We bring them together! They draw the aliens here!"

"Oh," Nevada said. "And then they grant your wish, right?" She looked at the henchmen who were parting for her like the Red Sea. "Everyone remember that part? Admittedly, it was a while back, if anyone wants to look it up on Wikipedia—"

"No!" Singh shrieked. "There's no wish! There's no first contact! We shoot them down."

Nevada stopped again. "Yeah, but what?" She resumed walking, muttering, "I am never going to get there at this rate…"

"It's genius in its simplicity!" Singh insisted. "The ship comes—"

"What ship?" Nevada interrupted.

"The mothership! The UFO! There's always a ship! We shoot it down and salvage the parts, advanced alien technology, a quantum leap in—"

"No, really, what are you going to do?"

"*I told you*!" Now Singh was screeching.

This time, Nevada resolved to keep moving, though she did puff out her cheeks and slowly exhale. "Okay. Cool, cool. Great stuff. I will just pick up the girl and we will be on our way, leave you to it!"

Inside the isolation chamber, Candice said, "Did she just call me 'the girl'?"

Singh gritted his teeth. The two bodyguards in front of him had their guns trained on Nevada from six feet away now. "You really think you can waltz in here, blow a hole in my boat, kill my men—then you take your girlfriend and leave?"

Nevada pointed at the detonator with her free hand. "Pretty much. I mean, it's not a *great* plan—there's no rockets *or* aliens—but I like it."

Singh shook his head. "How do I know you won't set off the charges when you leave?"

"I suppose you'll just have to hope I'm too pure of heart for such a nasty idea to even occur to me. Tell your dog to bring out my friend. I don't like being close enough to smell you."

Candice started to get to her feet, but Gore shoved her down again. "Nevada!" he shouted.

Nevada turned her head. "You better take your hand off her before she feels one drop of that skank-ass black sweat, Gore."

Gore gestured at her with the walkie-talkie in his hand. "It might interest you to know my men have a signal jammer onboard. Your detonator?" He shook his head. "It doesn't work anymore."

The guns came up again, a wall preventing her from going back, and then two executioners ahead in Singh's bodyguards.

Nevada stared down Singh with the full weight of her personality. She wasn't dealing with Gore; he was the lapdog. She was dealing with the purse strings. "You wanna take that chance?"

But even a mouse could only be pushed so far. "You always have been—what's the American expression? 'All hat and no cattle'?"

Nevada grinned. Hat, cattle—all she knew was that even a pair could beat a royal flush if the bluff was good enough. "Do you really think I would come in here all on my own, no backup?"

"Yes," Gore said bluntly.

"Well… I didn't."

"Oh, your friend on the boat?" Gore asked condescendingly. "Billings, hold up your walkie-talkie. Turn it to channel two."

One of Singh's bodyguards obediently held up his walkie-talkie. It chirped as Gore spoke through it. "Echo team, confirm target down."

A voice came over the radio with a slight tremble in it. "This is Echo 1. Target is down, objective is secure. No survivors."

Nevada's poker face didn't slip for an instant.

A mile away, in the hold of the *Blue Lagoon*, Butch pulled the walkie-talkie away from Echo 1—the last member of the fire team still standing.

"Good boy," he said when his finger was off the press-to-talk button. "I'm proud of you."

"What are you going to do to me?" Echo 1 asked.

"Well, that depends," Butch said. "Was my *Inception* steelbook blown up by a fucking mortar? Or not?"

He gave Echo 1 the same right hook that had once killed a man in the ring. And back then, he'd been wearing a boxing glove.

Butch turned the other way, going to get the M82a1 from the weapons rack when he spotted a stiff plastic bracelet on the floor—electromagnetic shark repellant.

"Hunh. Wonder if she needed that."

"Don't shoot her yet," Singh said. "I can't get blood on my clothes."

He pushed past the two bodyguards separating him from Nevada and smugly ripped the Steyr AUG away from her. Aiming the rifle around, he pantomimed shooting it.

"Bang! Bang! Pathetic." Singh tossed it aside. His voice boomed and his gestures were grand as he walked away from her. "Weapons and guns aren't the way of the future, Nevada. It's ideas! Vision!" He spun around, his sherwani swooshing around his thighs.

"It's ironic! All you've done for your child—but it's in dying, clearing the way for a new world order, that you've done him the greatest service of all. Under my stewardship, he'll live in a new Eden. I'll be nice and not mention you wanted to stop it all," Singh said. "I suppose that only leaves one question: Easy Nevada?"

"Yes?"

"No, Easy Nevada. I know that's not your real name. Out of all the names you could've chosen, why Easy Nevada?"

Nevada shrugged. "Joe Montana was taken."

Singh gestured understandingly. "Oh, right, the basketball player." He took a few more steps back until he was well and truly out of the splash zone. "Well, now all our cards are on the table."

Nevada scratched the back of her neck. "Yeah. Now we know where everyone stands." Glancing at the bodyguards with their guns trained at her, Nevada inched slightly toward them. She dug her pinky into her ear until she hit the earpiece. "Five feet in front of me. Butch, take 'em."

The .50 BMG round, designed to down airplanes, covered the distance—from where Butch had the M82a1 on a bipod to five feet in front of Nevada—at 2,799 feet per second. It burrowed through the *Liparus*'s double hull, into the hold, bringing its total transit time up to almost exactly two seconds before it hit the bodyguards holding Nevada at gunpoint. Then it was a bulldozer packed into a space as thick as a half-dollar. Between waist and sternum, the bodyguards ceased to exist except as red clouds.

It was a hell of a distraction.

Nevada sprinted for the isolation chamber, drawing her P210 and firing at the airlock control. The first round missed, but the second hit. The outer door started to close as Nevada barked, "Twenty feet to the left, fire for effect, fire for effect!"

Antimaterial rifle. Too bad for them they were made out of material.

Gore's men broke ranks and ran from the .50 rounds ripping through the hull like meteors, flying right through their midst. Some tried to block the gunfire with their ballistic shields, but that just meant they were lacerated by flying shards of metal at the same time as the .50 BMG blew through them. Others lost arms or legs, exploded more than severed, while the sheer force of the bullet's entry threw body and limb around like gale-force winds.

Nevada ignored all of that, putting all of herself into the run, covering the yards between herself and Candice like she could force the distance not to exist by will alone. The outer door hummed its last note as its electric motor propelled itself downward to close. Nevada threw herself down into a baseball slide, slipping under the door and coming up to her feet in the airlock. Her P210 was aimed at the inner door and Gore beyond it.

The door closed behind her. The airlock cycled and filtered the air inside it, bursts of nitrogenized air pushing against Nevada but not moving her gaze an inch.

"Do you ever walk into a room and just totally forget what you went in there to do?" Nevada asked.

Gore reached out to press the control on the inside. The jets of compressed gas shut off, leaving them both in silence. His black fingerprint stood out on the pristine white of the isolation chamber like mold on bread.

"It pauses," Gore explained. "Do you really think I'm going to let you ride off into the sunset with the girl while I bleed out?"

"You could always surrender," Nevada hinted.

"Not my style."

"Mine either. Guess that's how life gets to be so interesting." Nevada returned her gun to its holster. "How 'bout we settle this like John Wayne intended? You let the airlock do its thing. Door opens, we see who's the fastest hand in the West."

Candice couldn't contain herself any longer. "Be *careful,* Easy!" she cried.

Normally, Nevada would've felt irritation with anyone who felt the need to say something so obvious, or at least would've cracked a joke at that person's expense. She couldn't do that with Candice. What she'd said was just too sincere. As worried as she'd been about Candice, Candice was equally concerned about her. And there was a sweetness in that ache.

Nevada held up a comforting hand. "I'll just be a minute, baby. Mommy has to have a word with the nice man."

Sweat dripped from Gore's gun hand, pure black falling down to the floor and seeming to bubble there in its darkness. "I have a counterproposal."

"I'm listening."

"See, I'm not really a Western fan. Too old-fashioned for me. I'm more into that eighties stuff. You like *Die Hard*?"

"Classic," Nevada said. "Stone-cold."

"I don't know about that. To me, there's one glaring plot hole."

"Oh, really?" Nevada asked. "How are you wrong?"

Gore reached out to the glass between them, dotting its translucency with two smeared fingertips. "You've got Hans Gruber and John McClane." He added another finger, streaking its blackness beside the two already touching the glass. "Hans has McClane's wife and John's coming to save her. But it seems to me that no matter who wins the fight, that if Hans really wanted to ruin McClane's day, why, all he had to do was—"

Gore turned. His gun came up. Its barrel became level with Candice's belly, and he fired into Candice's stomach.

CHAPTER 15

Candice stood there, ignorant of how the bullet had lacerated her, crushed the flesh in its way, shoved it aside, and sent shockwaves tearing and separating through her physique. She felt a sharp jerk and knew she'd been shot, that it was the feeling of a bullet, but there wasn't pain. Only a coldness pressed against her body, going deeper and deeper.

She wanted to tell Nevada that it was okay, that it didn't hurt, that the wound couldn't be too bad if it didn't hurt. She didn't have a voice, though. The energy she'd always taken for granted—the ability to move and speak and even think, no matter how tired she was—it was no longer there. Heavy blankets wrapped around her, weighting her down, insulating her, mummifying her. Yet she didn't fall. She was still standing, watching as if through someone else's eyes while Gore reached out and pressed the door control. The airlock continued cycling, sounding far away. And she was still standing. A daughter of Meroe. Of Kush. Of the Sudan.

Nevada fired twice into the door, and even that was holding herself back too much. The glass spider-webbed but didn't break, so she slammed herself against it, bodily shaking the airlock, then driving her fist and the butt of the pistol against the glass until her knuckles stung. She heard the impact, bone on glass, but it didn't give. She kept hitting it anyway. She wouldn't say it felt good, but it was something, and she needed more *something* than *nothing* right then.

"You look like you wanna rip me apart with your bare hands." Gore dug his gun into its holster. "Feel free to try."

Blood prickled on Nevada's knuckles. She felt the weight of the P210 in her hand. It'd been a while since she'd really hated someone—needed them dead more than she wanted anything else. But she caught fire now like the forest after a long, dry summer.

She set the gun into its holster. "I'm gonna kill you a real bad kind of dead."

Nevada let the anger boil, let it burn, pushing it, stoking the flame. She needed it blue-hot like a welder's torch, stopped at the cusp of burning out of control, with the precision and accuracy to put all that heat where it would do the most good. The most damage.

"You really should've thought this through, Nevada," Gore said, teeth clenched, knuckles knotted up in fists. "This was just business. You made it personal. You thought you could be a hero? You're a hired gun, Nevada. A tool. Latex gloves. You're picked up, you're put to use, and then you're set aside. That's it. No grand destiny. No love story. Nothing special about you. You stand there and you look down on us, but what makes you any different from all the men you've killed today? What makes you so *great*?"

Candice barreled into him, digging her fingernails into his face, tearing five red furrows down his cheek. Gore staggered but quickly recovered; even as he howled in pain, he shoved Candice back. "Ungrateful bitch! I could've killed you quick!"

Candice landed sprawled on the ground, twisted in on herself. Nevada thought she could see how the bullet held itself inside her—pulling in at Candice like a hole letting out water. "You're right," Candice coughed, "I should be thanking you." She turned over. Not one part of her looked able to move except the hand with Gore's pistol in it. "For the gun."

Gore moved; Candice's finger twisted. He rocked back. Blood splashed behind him, sticking to the wall of the isolation chamber. He opened his mouth. Candice fired again. Gore took the next hit, and the next, and the next, his blood painting the wall behind him, but it was more like weights were being added to a scale than anything else.

When Candice's stolen gun clicked empty, he was still standing.

His chest red, his hands stigmata black, Gore took a step, then pitched forward with that last gasp of energy, landing flat on his face. Exit wounds had made a ravaged no-man's-land of his back. His forefinger twitched, nail scratching at the floor, a streak of black, and then the only thing moving was the blood pouring from him.

Almost like an afterthought, the airlock finally opened. Nevada flooded inside, jumping Gore's body, dropping to her knees beside Candice and pushing her hand into the blood, the dwindling heat. She could smell the cordite where Candice had been shot.

"That was some shooting," Nevada babbled, ripping at Candice's clothing to bunch it over the wound. "Good grouping, *great* consistency—when was the last time you went to the range?"

"Thea..."

Nevada gritted her teeth. That couldn't be it—couldn't be the last time Candice said her name, moved her lips that way. "Come on, now. You're not going to actually make me tell you to stay with me and not go to sleep and all the clichés... You know all that. You're smart, you're PhD girl. Don't tell me you slept with the professor or something."

Hundreds of bullets crashed into the isolation chamber, shredding the airlock, chipping away at the reinforced glass, filling the room with a cacophony. Nevada turned: Singh had rallied the troops, forming a firing line, every gun pouring bullets at her and Candice while the launcher trudged down the tracks, approaching the open bow. Outside there were colors Nevada had never seen the sky hold before.

Candice's hand touched her face. Cold but soft. Nevada remembered the tremendous effort, the sheer will she had seen in Candice when she'd shot Gore. Now she was exerting herself even more, just to feel this. Her.

Nevada clasped Candice's hand against her cheek and buried her lips in it. She could smell Candice, sweet and true and without a hint of the blood, not yet.

"You have to stop him," Candice said.

"No, fuck that. Don't worry about that. I'm getting you out of here."

"I'm not going anywhere." Candice shut her eyes. Nevada could see what an effort it was to open them again.

She brushed a lock of hair back from her face, suddenly realizing this was what Candice was trying so hard to see—bloodied and bruised and the wrong shade of lipstick. Not worthy of her.

"I came here for you," Nevada insisted. "You hear me? You. That's all."

She heard glass shatter, a bullet hum and ping into the chamber. Strong as the walls were, nothing could take the sheer destructive force that was being unleashed now. Sooner or later, it would all be gone.

"He has a tablet on him. Launches the missile," Candice pressed. Her voice was fragile, on the verge of shattering. "Get the tablet."

"Why?" Nevada demanded. "Why should I give a shit, huh? What do I care if he wants to blow up some fucking—some—God, Candice, don't *do this to me.*"

"You care because you're a good person." Candice coughed. Nevada shut her eyes. "And because Singh is a fucking wanker. Go kick his arse."

"Ah, geez, how am I supposed to say no to you when you talk dirty?"

Nevada looked frantically around the hold. She could tell Butch to fire on the men blowing the isolation chamber apart, but there were at least a dozen of them—no way Butch could pick all of them off. Not to mention the bullets would probably go through them and kill her and Candice even sooner. Maybe she could take out Singh or better yet, the rocket, but she didn't trust their game of telephone to hit a relatively fast-moving target like that. Maybe when it came to a stop, but Nevada doubted they would last that long.

"Any chance Singh owes you a favor?" Nevada asked. "If that rocket stopped for just five seconds..."

Candice grinned, put so much effort into forming the expression that it looked like it hurt her cheeks. "They have a spare."

Nevada could only look at her for a moment. "God, I love you." Then she turned around, scanning the hold—she couldn't imagine it would be too hard to make out; the room was one big metal space. There, something under a tarp at the aft side of the hold. She could only imagine her luck that she hadn't set it off when she'd blown her way into the hold. Desperately interlocking the fingers of her left hand with Candice's, Nevada brought her right hand up and fingered her earpiece. "Butch, you copy?"

"Five by five."

"Listen to me very carefully," Nevada said, orienting herself to face the tarp, carefully calculating the distance to it, all while trying to ignore the bullets crashing into the isolation chamber, wearing it down to nothing. "Four hundred and thirty feet in front of me, adjust fire."

"Shot, over."

And Nevada watched for a bullet hole to pop through the hull, watched for the impact on that fucking tarp...

"I can't help but think this would be easier using the metric system," Candice muttered.

Nevada saw the split-second replacement of unbroken hull with a puckered curling of metal. The round come so close, the tarp actually fluttered—

Singh must've heard the thundercrack of it. "What are you doing? What are you doing?"

"Add four, left three!" Nevada shouted.

Another bullet broke through the glass; Nevada felt the wind of its passage.

Singh dismounted the launcher, running to scoop up a rifle from a fallen man. "Get her. Get her now!"

Thunder roared. A shower of sparks as the .50 BMG round broke through the hull and hit the tarp. Nevada could've sworn she heard something hissing. She threw herself over Candice, covering her ears—

"It's a dud!" Singh shouted.

The blast could be felt through the entire ship, shredding right through the hull, almost breaking the tanker in half. It was so powerful that outside the hull, it knocked the water back in a foaming sphere for a full five seconds, like a fist rearing back to throw a punch. The top of the sphere breached the surface, sending a plume of water into the air that towered above Butch on the *Blue Lagoon*—the Niagara turned momentarily upside down.

"What the fuck are they putting in bullets these days?" he asked.

Then the water rushed back in, filling the abandoned space and then gaining new ground, rushing into the *Liparus* like a starving animal scenting prey…

The sheer force of the explosion, even from so far away, knocked Singh unconscious. He was woken by the sound of groaning metal—the *Liparus* in its death throes—reverberating in the cold metal floor under him. He picked himself up slowly, gingerly, his innards *hurting* with the pressure blast that had run through them. It felt like all of him had been punched by an enormous fist.

Then he discovered the floor was *tilting*. Only by degrees, but as water flooded into not only the hold but also the pump room and the engine room and everywhere else Nevada had left exposed by blowing a hole between the two segments of the ship...

It was sinking. The boat's aft was being weighed down by water, pulling it below the waves, and the bow drew upward, actually up into the air, as the counterbalance of the waterlogged aft grew heavier and heavier.

That was the last straw for the men. They openly fled, dropping their guns and ballistic shields to pile onto the elevator.

"Cowards!" Singh roared, firing his rifle after them.

A few bullets actually hit, bright red holes appearing in the back of one of the men. Most only ran faster, but a few turned and fired back.

Singh ran for the only cover available—the launcher—still crawling into position. "Stop shooting at me! I'm shooting at you!" he snapped as he threw himself behind the launcher.

He tried to fire more at them, but the rifle was empty and he hadn't brought any additional ammo. The ship continued to slant—it was now at a ten-degree angle. Singh wouldn't be able to make the uphill climb for much longer. He started to panic but then realized there was a simple solution. There was a gantry in back of the launcher, like the balcony on the back of a train caboose where a politician might give a stump speech.

Singh hauled himself into the cradle formed by the gantry's safety railing. No matter how the ship angled itself, the railing would keep him from falling. He could ride it all the way to launch position.

Huddling in the corner of the gantry, Singh checked the tablet Gore had given him. As he might've guessed, the sinking ship was playing havoc with the missile's telemetry. It couldn't safely fire yet, not without risking hitting the inside of the *Liparus* and making this all for nothing. Singh would have to let the launcher move further, then launch.

Already he could see the target coming into focus through the open bow—it wasn't a saucer, not quite, more like a mandala, endless concentric circles forming some sort of pattern. It made his eyes hurt. He didn't like it. He would fire the missile at it point-blank if he had to. Then he'd think of a way off the sinking ship. Something would come to him. It always did.

The blast whitened out every window of the isolation chamber, glass crunching and grinding together, but that didn't matter now. There was no one left to break it.

Nevada pulled herself up, bruised and wincing, feeling a burning trickle of blood running down her forehead. This, she thought, might not have been one of her better ideas. Still, she keyed the earpiece.

"Good fucking kill, Butch."

Static greeted her. She could only assume some of the delicate inner workings of the miniaturized radio had been damaged in the blast. She could sympathize. Her stomach felt like it had been used as a basketball.

"Are you okay?" Candice asked. Her voice sounded nothing like her—more like an old woman's.

"I'm fine," Nevada said. "Think I just had some British cooking and forgot about it."

Candice laughed and winced in equal measure. "It hurts when I laugh, you tosser."

Nevada looked around. Good news: no one was shooting at them anymore. Bad news: the good news was because the ship was taking on water. She stripped off her bulletproof vest, struggling into the sleeves of her wetsuit instead. The vest would only drag her down; the wetsuit would give her some protection against the water's chill.

And what's going to protect your ass from the sharks? Nevada looked to the stern of the boat as it came down like an overbalanced scale. The bodies and body parts of the dead had relocated, giving the swirling water a distinct red tinge that the circling shark fins looked all too at home in.

"Nevada," Candice whispered, or maybe that was just her speaking voice now.

Nevada looked at her. Candice was too weak to point, so Nevada followed her gaze to the missile launcher, dragging its way up the track despite the growing slant against it. Was it set to launch when it reached the end of the track? Nevada glanced at Candice again. It was obvious she wouldn't want Nevada to take that chance.

"I will be right back," Nevada promised, pressing a quick kiss to Candice's forehead.

"Okay, I'll wait," Candice replied, her tone so dry it maybe could've made the *Liparus* seaworthy again.

Stumbling and limping her way across the slanting deck, Nevada got to the inner door and hit the control where Gore's black fingerprint marked it. The outermost portion of the airlock had shielded her side from harm; the inner door confidently opened, not registering that the outer door had been eaten away by the barrage. Nevada easily stepped over it, but her foot landed wrong on the other side. She tripped, landing hard on her shoulder, and skittered down with the slick pull of gravity.

Teeth grinding together, Nevada fought her way up, digging her heels in, scrambling and clawing her way across the deck and its fifty-degree angle until she reached the track. There, she finally managed to latch onto the ties between the railings. They formed a ladder, letting her pull herself up after the launcher as fast as she could go. Nevada didn't dare look over her shoulder at the isolation chamber. She would only see the water rising up to engulf it.

The launcher loomed up ahead of her, close enough for her to hear the whine of its engine even over the roaring water. She thrust herself up to it, grabbing onto the railing, heaving herself onto the gantry.

Suddenly Singh was there, coming out from behind the missile to swing a rifle at her. Nevada turned her head at the last moment. The butt of the rifle smashed into her brow, hurtling her to the floor of the gantry. Nevada heard a sharp crack ringing in her ears as she went down. She couldn't imagine her skull's resale value hadn't just gone down.

"You stupid cunt!" Singh roared. "Do you know what you've done?"

"No, but hum a few bars and I'll fake it."

Even with her head pounding like a snare drum, Nevada heard the rifle swinging down again. She rolled to the side; it crashed into the flooring next to her, the resin stock cracking from the impact. Nevada lashed out with her foot. She caught Singh in the shin, but she'd been barefoot since she took off her flippers. All she accomplished was making Singh fall to his knees. The tablet slipped out of his waistband and bounced off the floor, catching between two of the guardrails.

Nevada's head felt like it would split open. She pulled herself up, facing Singh from the left side of the gantry. He staggered to his feet as well. Both of them eyed the tablet, lost in the six feet of space between them.

Singh tightened his grip on the rifle's barrel. "You should've joined me, Nevada. We could've ruled together as gods!"

Nevada paused. "You didn't ask."

Singh's face assumed a quizzical expression. "Oh. Right. Well, fuck you anyway!"

"No, fuck you!" Nevada replied, hand shooting for her holstered gun.

Singh swung the rifle quicker—the butt crashed like a wrecking ball into her upper arm, cracking the bone, leaving Nevada's fingers rubber on the grip of her pistol. She went southpaw instead, throwing all her strength into a left uppercut to make Singh cough up his ribs. It lifted Singh off his feet and left him falling back against the railing on the right.

The tablet trembled with the force of their footfalls, slipping back and forth.

Singh's voice was so reedy, it seemed to cut its way out of him. "I will kill everything you love," he vowed.

"Good luck," Nevada told him. "I love like three things in the world, and one of them is cheese."

Singh threw the rifle at her. Nevada instinctively turned, bracing her shoulder to take the brunt of the impact. The rifle painfully bounced off her, but Singh was right behind it, tackling her down and spinning her so she was facing away from him.

Hooking one arm around the railing, he shoved her down into it, cutting off her air with a guardrail against her throat. Nevada pushed back, throwing her good arm backward, jabbing her elbow into his midsection. But Singh was enraged, insane, shrugging off the blows as he pushed her down harder. Nevada felt her vertebra cracking under the pressure…

She got her foot up, coiling it against the railing and then pushing off hard, sending them both across the gantry. They struck the tablet as they flew backwards, sending it spinning—then Singh's spine crashed into the right-hand railing. Nevada felt the heat of the gasp that was driven out of him.

He held onto her like a vise, snaking his arms around her throat, tightening his grip to grind the life out of her. Nevada tried elbowing him again. At this point, she must've crushed his ribs into dust, emptied his liver and spleen and kidneys like tubes of toothpaste, but he wouldn't let go. He wanted every last drop of life in her; he wouldn't let go…

"You're fired, Nevada," he spat. "You're fucking *fired*!"

Nevada forced herself forward, dragging Singh's weight on top of her own. Her vision was darkening; she groped half-blind for the tablet at her feet. Finally came up with it. Singh's bulk was too much for her. She fell against the left-hand railing. Singh was all over her, legs around her midriff, arm around her throat, the hand in her hair pushing her into the chokehold that was forcing every last breath out of her.

Nevada made herself focus. The tablet. The controls. The green fucking button.

She pressed it.

The freezing temperature that'd come in with the floodwater instantly skyrocketed, becoming the muggiest summer day Nevada had ever felt. She heard a roar slowly gathering, eclipsing the blood pounding in her ears, and then Singh let out a shriek. The missile was launching, its exhaust hissing right into Singh's body. He tried to move, but Nevada dug her fingers into the arm he had around her throat, holding him right there, a human shield protecting her from the fury of the launch.

Then the missile was gone and she was throwing her head back, ending Singh's scream with a broken nose, spinning, throwing him off her and off the gantry. She watched him burn on the way down. He splashed into the rising water with a puff of steam.

"You can't fire me," Nevada breathed. "I quit."

She looked at the tablet in her hand. Pressed the red button with her thumb.

Nothing happened. The missile kept going, shooting up the nearly vertical hold, almost to the open bow—

Nevada thumbed the red button again. Again. Cursing, she rubbed the tablet's screen against her belly, hoping the wetsuit was dry enough to clean it off, then thumbed the red button once more.

The missile's jets cut off. It hung there in space, gravity catching up with it, before plummeting back into the hold. Nevada ducked. It bounced off the floor's steep slope once, then shot over Nevada's head, a big dumb hunk of metal crashing down into the ocean.

"Fucking touchscreens."

The ripples from the impact covered and uncovered a small, flailing form in the water. Singh. Burnt, blackened, he kicked at the swirling water, staying at the surface like a tumor that just wouldn't be a good skin cell and die.

"Nevada! Nevada! You can't stop this! This is my destiny!"

From on high, Nevada could see what he couldn't. Shadowy forms in the water with him. Slate-gray fins knifing through the water. "You want destiny? Here it fucking comes."

Singh jerked underwater; popped back up. A nibble—a taste test. Then he was grabbed in earnest, pulled screaming through the water with jaws clamped on his lower body. He beat weakly at the shark, then clawed at the water like he could find a handhold on it, but there was no escaping the blood billowing all around him. As he was dragged one way, another fin came from the opposite direction. Ships passing in the night.

Nevada saw the second great white come up, eyes rolling back, teeth jagged and endless. Then it had as much hold on Singh's torso as the first shark had on his legs. Whatever happened to him then was thankfully lost in a cloud of spreading crimson.

Nevada tossed the tablet down into the water with him.

She took off at a run, leaping the railing and making a few steps on the sloped floor before gravity took her. Skidding downward, she aimed herself at the isolation chamber and braced her legs—the impact shattered the wall of the chamber completely, carrying her inside. Thankfully, the next wall stopped her descent. Aching, her brain on fire, her lungs never getting enough air, she picked her way over to Candice.

She was the most beautiful woman Nevada had ever seen and she looked like hell.

"Easy," Candice whispered. "Are you okay? You're bleeding."

Nevada touched the side of her head; it was slick with blood. "I'll be fine. How are you?"

"How do I look?"

"Pale," Nevada said. "I didn't want to say anything, but if you ever wanted to be part of a country club, now's a good time."

Shuddering, groaning metal was all around them. The hull of the *Liparus* couldn't take the stress it was under. Nevada saw it buckling, tearing itself apart under its own weight.

"Thanks for coming," Candice said.

"I wouldn't miss it."

"I'm glad… I just wanted to see you again. I'm happy to see you again."

Cracks radiated through the hull to the sound of screaming metal, widening the breach that had already killed the ship. Nevada laid down beside Candice. She couldn't think. She didn't know what to do. She'd never thought the scent of seawater could be so overpowering.

"Talk to me, Easy," Candice said. "You know how many times I've wanted to hear your voice?"

"What do you wanna talk about?" Nevada asked.

"Anything. Even Spider-Man."

Nevada felt her lips twisting almost against her will. "How about you?"

"What about me?"

Nevada laughed. *That* struck her as funny—maybe she'd finally gotten hit on the head one too many times. "What *about* you? Candice… Candice…" Nevada shut her eyes, wincing as rivets popped somewhere, echoing as they ricocheted off the hull. "After I gave up the baby, I went to war with myself. I hated myself for giving him up, and I tried to love myself. I told myself I wouldn't be a good mother, and then I told myself I was… Easy Nevada. Then I met you. And there was this calm."

"Like you weren't afraid?"

Nevada shook her head. "I'm terrified, Candice. I'm so used to the chaos that anything else scares the shit out of me. But you make me brave too. I don't want the chaos anymore. I want you."

Candice didn't answer. She was beyond answering—a still, small thing that was so very *her*, even now, in the middle of all this. Nevada forced herself to move, muscles protesting, bones feeling like they were in pieces already. But she managed to get her good arm around Candice, to pull her into her lap.

Above, the sky was an alien color—a halo on the world. Nevada looked up at the nimbus. The gears that spun the world laid bare. The thing that made the sun rise after it set. The place love went when it wasn't in people anymore. Or maybe she just had a concussion.

"Hey," Nevada croaked—she barely recognized her own voice. "You! Up there! I don't know what you are… I don't care. You got what you wanted. The skulls are here. Take 'em. But the way I see it, you owe me. You. Owe. Me. So fix her. Don't let her die, and we'll call it even." She coughed. Tasted blood. "Don't make me come up there."

Metal screamed on all sides. The *Liparus* broke in two, their half falling from vertical to horizontal. Nevada held tight to Candice as the shattered husk crashed down into the water. *Stay with me, stay with me, stay with me.* She didn't know if she was saying it or thinking it. The noise was overpowering; she was a note of music in a cacophony. But the metal stopped groaning and the water stopped roaring. There was a kind of calm. With the *Liparus* open both at the site of the split and at its bow, the water wasn't rushing in, just filling the halved boat up as it fell.

"Yes."

Nevada followed the word like it was one more treasure to track down, but there was no need to search. Candice was in her arms, hale and healthy, a slice of midnight in the middle of all the sunlight that'd been let in.

"What?"

"Yes," Candice repeated. "You asked me to stay. Remember?"

Nevada pulled aside the wad of makeshift bandages she'd pushed into Candice's wound. Under it, there was unbroken skin, marred only by the dried blood. And even that couldn't do much to diminish the perfection of her voluptuous breasts, which Nevada now realized she'd ripped through Candice's shirt to expose.

"I won't ruin the moment if you won't," Candice said.

"Deal," Nevada said. "Though are near-death experiences really cold? I'm only—"

A gun barked once, twice, three times, bullets shattering the panes of glass beside them. Nevada whirled, shielding Candice with her body. She tried to go for her gun, but her arm was still broken—all trying to move it did was send a bolt of agony through her already hurting body.

Gore stood over them, his chest stained black with drying blood, more streaking out of his mouth and down his chin. His gun aimed at Nevada now, a syringe drawing the fear out of her and filling Gore with sadistic joy. A dying man's last request.

"Singh is dead," Nevada said. "It's over. No one's paying you anymore."

"You think I care about that?" Gore limped forward through the rising water, blood trailing off his legs with each dragging step. "No. No, I'm going to kill you, Nevada. Not because it's my job, not because I'm getting paid, but because you are just so—*fucking*—annoying!"

The harpoon speared into Gore, ripping him sideways to slam into what had once been the floor and pinning him there like a collected butterfly. The gun was jarred out of his hand. Gore could only hang there, impaled, stuck in place as the ship slowly sank.

"Try sharing a bunk bed with her," Butch said from the prow of the *Blue Lagoon*, letting go of the harpoon gun.

CHAPTER 16

Ten minutes later, they were leaving the *Liparus* to its watery grave. None of them saw any sign of the skulls. If they were still there, they'd gone down with the ship. Sunken treasure.

They also left behind an entire flotilla of lifeboats, including the launch that Butch set adrift with four very unconscious bodies onboard. But if any of Gore's men shared his post-Singh sentiments, they weren't about to act on it. The *Blue Lagoon* left them to go ashore while it headed out to sea.

"Thank *you*," Butch said, taking back the P210 and returning it to its place on the gun rack. "You finally got one of these back to me. All it took was someone breaking your gun hand."

Nevada grimaced. Her broken arm was in a sling now, not to mention the bandage wrapped around her head. Mild concussion, Butch had told her.

"My gun hand's fine," she said. "Aiming just might be a problem for a while."

"Maybe you should take a break from shooting people," Candice suggested.

"Or teach yourself to be ambidextrous," Butch said. "When your right arm heals, you can shoot with two guns at once. You'd save money in the long run. So many of these gun stores, you buy one pistol, you get the second half off. Pays for itself eventually."

"Oh God," Candice said. "There are two of them."

Thunder crashed, pulling everyone's attention to the darkening sky ahead. Butch refocused his attention on the controls, Nevada joining him to look over the readout.

"We have a problem?" she asked.

"Nothing the *Blue Lagoon* can't handle," Butch assured her. "But would you mind going to the engine room and making sure the thing doesn't—you know—the thing?"

Nevada rolled her eyes. "Most people, their engine breaks, they replace it, y'know."

"The engine is not broken," Butch stressed. "It's *interesting*."

Nevada rolled her eyes again, this time adding a groan as she went below decks to the engine room.

Inside, the engine let out a rolling, clattering, somehow reassuring rattle. Nevada glanced over the gauges and dials before she noticed that Candice had followed her.

"Hey."

"Hey."

The *Blue Lagoon* burst through a swell, rolling them both for a staggering moment. They regained their footing. Candice laughed a little.

"You might want to buckle up back there!" Butch yelled through the hatch. "We're going to be having some of that global warming weather, so if either of you used hairspray, that's on you."

Nevada passed Candice, banging her fist on the bulkhead to signal Butch. "Hey, Bro, give us a moment, okay?"

"Okay! I'll just keep busy not letting us drown!"

Nevada looked apologetically at Candice. "He might've been adopted, but I don't think even my parents would've picked him."

Candice smiled. "He's not so bad. Anyway, I got used to you."

Another wave pitched the boat from side to side. Nevada caught Candice as she stumbled and helped her down onto a workbench. They held themselves down by holding onto the edges of the table. It gave Nevada something to do with her hand.

"So," Nevada said. "Aliens."

"Yes!" Candice cried. "I rather figured it was extraterrestrial technology, once I realized how advanced the skulls really were, and the archaeological record simply doesn't support a *terrestrial* civilization of that caliber, so I reasoned it had to be… well, aliens."

Nevada shrugged. "Yeah, I met a woman who told me it was aliens. I forget her name."

Candice's lips curdled. "I think technically they're extradimensional beings—not from space, but from the space *between* spaces..."

Nevada smiled fondly. "You are such a know-it-all."

"I am not!" Candice protested.

"You're right, you're not," Nevada said.

"And what's that supposed to mean?"

Nevada turned to her. "What would you do if I kissed you right now?"

Candice smiled at her. "I have no idea."

"Let's find out."

The last time they'd kissed, Nevada could've sworn she'd memorized every detail of Candice's lips: the taste, the feel, the surprising heat under that genteel exterior that dragged Nevada away from all self-control. She might not have forgotten anything, but she still wasn't prepared for what she felt: the gratitude on both their parts—for finding her, for being there—a thankfulness, an appreciation that grew every second they had each other until another wave rolled the boat and they were both pitched down to the floor.

Nevada barely even felt it.

"I knew it," she said.

"Knew what?" Candice asked.

"You'd fall hopelessly in love with me."

Candice purred with sympathy. "You just now noticed?"

The ship pitched again, rolling them over one another, Candice on top, then Nevada, but all she could care about was the kiss.

An hour later, the storm was over. Butch's foot was up, and the prosthetic one lay on the deck. He only took a passing interest in the controls, but when Candice and Nevada emerged from the engine room, his expression curdled.

"Oh, *gross.*"

"Hey! Don't be rude," Nevada chided him.

Candice leaned over to her. "He does know you're..."

Butch sat up. "No, hey, no, don't get me wrong. I'm not prejudiced. We're all a little bit gay."

"Butch, I've seen your jorts," Nevada said, "you're not even a little bit gay."

"I'm just saying, Candice Cushing, you're a *doctor*. You can do way better. I once saw Easy drop a slice of lasagna on the floor; she picked it up and ate it. And it fell on the carpet."

Candice's gaze flew to Nevada. "The carpet?"

"It was well within the five-second rule." Nevada bent over the GPS unit. "What's our bearing?"

"Well, we're five days out from nowhere in particular, and if anyone asks, we didn't see anyone sink an oil tanker."

"We could always blame it on Greenpeace."

"By the way," Butch said, opening up a drawer and going for a satellite phone. "Jacques called."

Nevada's brow furrowed. "Jacques? What'd he want?"

Butch tossed her the satphone. "Probably wants to know if you know anyone selling a plane on the cheap. Get his *Tailspin* thing back up and running."

"*Tailspin*?" Candice asked as Nevada dialed.

"It's this old cartoon show." Though he spoke to Candice, Butch's eyes followed Nevada as she disappeared down into the crew quarters. "You know the characters from *The Jungle Book*? Baloo, Shere Khan, King Louie? Well, imagine they're all in this 1930s, dieselpunk kinda setting. Baloo is like this Han Solo type who flies a seaplane for hire, Louie owns a bar he goes to, Khan is this evil Lex Luthor kinda guy he works for sometimes... Now that I think about it, this is a really weird premise for a children's cartoon."

They heard Nevada sit down heavily on the bottom step of the staircase. Candice looked at Butch. He gestured back at her, indicating that he was piloting the boat. So Candice went down the steps herself.

Hearing them creak, Nevada scooted over, making room for Candice to sit down beside her.

"Everything okay?"

"Everything's fine." Nevada sounded shell-shocked, her voice a monotone. "Jacques is in the hospital, a real hospital. He's healing nicely. And my kid..." She shook her head. "*The* kid... He has forty percent less of a tumor than he had yesterday."

Candice's eyebrows jolted up. "That's good news, then. Right? Right?"

Nevada nodded vacantly. "That's very good news. Very good news..."

"So?" Candice prompted.

"So?"

"What do you want to do now?"

Nevada thrust up her shoulders in a shrug so hard that her broken arm made her wince. "I have no idea. I've been doing this shit so long, I have no idea what I'm doing when I'm not doing this."

Candice rested her head against Nevada's shoulder, reaching over to squeeze her leg. "Maybe we could just stay out here a while. Enjoy being adrift some."

"Yeah... That sounds nice... Candice?"

"Yeah, Easy?"

"Do you know anyone selling a plane on the cheap?" Nevada's face cracked into a grin. "It's for a friend." Then Nevada's charm was derailed by a huge yawn. She waved it off apologetically. "Sorry, sorry. It's not you. It's just the adrenaline wearing off. And now I want to sleep for a million years."

Candice reached out to grip her arm. "Wait a minute: you have a concussion. You really shouldn't go to sleep."

Nevada's tongue briefly probed the inside of her cheek. "No? What should I do, then?"

Candice gave her arm a squeeze. "Stay awake. Find some way to stimulate yourself..."

"I can hear you," Butch interrupted. "It's not a big boat."

"Love wins, Butch," Nevada replied.

"Please, by all means, go and have sex, but don't make me listen to you two useless lesbians spitting game at each other. It's like watching Taylor Swift do a collab with the Wu-Tang Clan."

"That's a horrible metaphor," Candice said.

"Yeah," Nevada nodded, "I would totally watch that."

EPILOGUE

DO NOT LOOK FOR THE WRECKAGE. DO NOT GO NEAR THE CARGO.

Candice woke up covered in sweat. It took her a moment to gather herself, but she did. She could see Nevada. She knew she was safe. The only thing pressing in on her was the calming serenity of her surroundings, like bandages around her body, letting her heal.

It'd been a week since the *Liparus* had sunk, and they were still lying low, though in Nevada's world, that was little different than being on holiday. Butch had dropped them off in Zanzibar, Pemba Island, where Nevada had a standing reservation at the Manta Resort. As she put it, the night manager owed her a favor. She had once kept certain photographs from being sent to the newspapers, and he was grateful. So grateful that he overlooked how Nevada had kept the photographs from being sent by not mailing them after she'd had them developed.

Their room at the Manta was, on the surface, a cabin. Literally. It floated above the coral reef that surrounded Pemba Island, a wooden three-story that went from rooftop deck to sea level lounge to the bedroom underwater. Windows surrounded the bed, letting in the vibrant colors of the reef and the endless variety of fish that called it home.

It was a spectacular view, a two-thousand-dollar-a-night view, and Candice's eyes still went to Nevada, who stood at the foot of the bed, looking out at a swirling school of yellowtail fusilier shimmering outside the window. All she wore was the cast on her fractured arm.

Candice had always found Nevada attractive, but there was the technical knowledge that she was all toned muscle and an all-over tan and arms that really should be illegal. And then there was knowing how Nevada felt under her, how she purred when Candice's tongue traveled over her nipple, how she tasted, how she *came*...

Candice threw back the sheet and got out of bed. She was suddenly very, very glad she didn't have to pretend she wasn't attracted to Nevada anymore.

Thanks to the reflection in the glass, she could see Nevada's face, see Nevada see her body. See the grin on Nevada's face as Candice got closer and closer, until her arms were wrapped around Nevada.

"Two thousand dollars a night," Candice breathed in Nevada's ear. "You really wanna spend it looking at fish?"

"I was thinking." Nevada turned her head until Candice could kiss her. "You always say I should think things through more."

"And what were you thinking about? How good you look?"

"No." Nevada bowed her head to kiss the arm Candice had around her chest. "I have you to do that for me."

Candice buried her embarrassed grin in the back of Nevada's neck. "You do have me. So you *could* stop trying to be so cool. What were you thinking about? Really?"

"That it is much better to not know what to do with your life with tequila than it is to not know what to do with your life with tap water."

Candice kissed Nevada's cheek. Then licked it. And as a flush spread over Nevada's chest, she left her to pick the bottle up from beside the bed.

"Not to be insensitive—" she began, pouring for them.

"Oh, please, I'd love to see what your version of insensitivity looks like."

Candice handed over Nevada's glass. "You went through all of this to save someone. You ever think he might want to meet you?"

Nevada drank before answering. "He has a life. He has a family. Me, I'd just... confuse him." She brightened. "And it really wouldn't be fair to his mom, since I'm definitely cooler than her."

"Okay."

"She probably drives a minivan. Wears cardigans. That's not my life."

"What is?" Candice asked.

"Right now? Watching you take a sip." Nevada clinked her glass against Candice's. "Come on—you know how angry Butch is going to be when he finds out I stole that bottle from him? Make it worth my while."

Candice took a sip. By now, she could imbibe with barely even a coughing fit. "Ghastly," she exhaled afterward.

Nevada rubbed her back supportively. "We'll make a badass out of you yet."

"Excuse me? Which of us killed a yuppie, and which of us killed a—Navy SEAL?"

"You mostly killed him," Nevada reasoned. "Not to take away from that, but Butch had to finish him off."

"Didn't the sharks have to finish Singh off?"

Nevada's jaw fell for a moment. As long as her mouth was open, she put some more tequila in it. "Well, I like sharks. You know the great white is kinda like a dinosaur? It's been around for millions of years without evolving. Everyone else either died out or became some bitch-ass bird."

"Sharks and tequila," Candice mused. "Is there anything you like that can't get you killed?"

"You."

Candice's eyes flashed dangerously. "What makes you think I can't get you killed?"

"If you haven't by now, I must be invincible."

"I'd imagine invincibility would come with a little more stamina." Candice grinned at Nevada's look. "Two thousand dollars a night," she reminded her.

"I'm not looking at fish," Nevada retorted.

"No, but if all you're going to do is look…"

"Finish your drink," Nevada told her. "You might need a little liquid courage for this."

Thirty minutes and four fingers later, Candice was covered in sweat again. She rested against the window, letting the cool glass relieve the heat, even if Nevada kept stirring it up again—brushing her hand against Candice's thigh like there was anything more she could get out of a body that had already exploded.

"I hate to nag—" Candice panted.

"That's a lie."

"I strongly dislike to nag," Candice said pointedly, "but before I start to worry, any idea what to do next?"

"Fisting," Nevada said bluntly.

"I meant for work."

"Well, I wouldn't feel right if you paid me for it, but I suppose I could accept a tip."

"I actually do have a tip for you—wine is more romantic than tequila. And now I'm getting cold…"

Candice started to get up, but Nevada said, "Uh-uh." She rearranged herself to be sitting against the window glass, pulling Candice into her lap and wrapping her arms around her. Candice sighed. That did feel nicely warm. And the way Nevada touched her face, being so gentle with the same hand that had just been so…assertive? Candice wouldn't put a word to it, but she didn't ever want to leave. And she could tell Nevada didn't ever want to let her go.

"Trophy wife," Nevada said.

"Trophy wife?" Candice repeated.

"I think I'd be good at it. Drinking margaritas at noon. Taking my Pomeranian to a spa. Selling Mary Kay products." Nevada snapped her fingers. "That's it!"

"Mary Kay products? I thought we agreed, love, no more working for supervillains."

Nevada quickly gulped down the sip of tequila she'd taken. "No, no, I just remembered who told me about the aliens. Lady Tendai! Like the crappy Spider-Man chick?"

Candice heaved a sigh and set down her glass. "Easy, I have listened to you complain about Spider-Man movies for a solid month now. And you know what?"

"What?" Nevada asked, taking another gulp.

"I'm not saying their mischaracterization of Mary Jane Watson is the least of the Tom Holland movies' problems, because I actually do find it offensive that the only thing this Michelle character has in common with the real Mary Jane is that they're both Peter Parker's love interests, like it's 2020 and we're really defining female characters entirely by their relationship to a man? But! But! Those movies have a lot of other problems too! Spider-Man is supposed to be his own man, yet they pretty much make him a sidekick to Iron Man! He's supposed to be a working-class hero, but at any time he can just ask Tony to float him a million dollars and his money troubles are over! He has a billion-dollar suit with an AI—" Candice paused, noticing Nevada was staring at her. "What?"

"Marry me," Nevada said.

OTHER BOOKS FROM YLVA PUBLISHING

www.ylva-publishing.com

PRIMAL TOUCH

Amber Jacobs

ISBN: 978-3-95533-858-9
Length: 255 pages (99,000 words)

Rumors of a rare, white tiger have lured wildlife photographer Ashley Richards deep into the Indian jungle. There, she crosses paths with a ruthless poacher and Leandra, a mysterious, feral woman, who seems at one with the fierce felines she protects. In this charged, exotic, lesbian romance, Ashley faces danger, a deadly vendetta, and the clash of two worlds, which changes everything she knows.

NEVER TOO LATE FOR HEROES

(The Superheroine Collection)

A.L.Brooks

ISBN: 978-3-96324-343-1
Length: 290 pages (96,0000 words)

Agent Geena Fox's secret lover died six years ago facing down the supervillain, Jewel. Now Geena's stuck with Leigh, a new rookie with a nose for trouble. Meanwhile, over in a retirement home, four mystery women are making trouble of their own. What do they know?

A cracking adventure with a side of romance for lovers of tough, jaded cops, lesbians, superheroes, evil villains, and feisty retirees.

ABOUT GEORGETTE KAPLAN

It was never easy for Georgette Kaplan. She was born a poor child in Mississippi, where she still remembers sitting on the porch with her family, singing and dancing around her. After learning she was adopted, at the age of 21 she hitchhiked to St. Louis, where she worked at a gas station and in a traveling carnival. After a shooting incident at the gas station, she decided to quit and pursue her lifelong dream of a career in writing. She now lives back in Mississippi with her life partner Marie.

CONNECT WITH GEORGETTE
Tumblr: georgettekaplan.tumblr.com
E-Mail: kaplangeorgette@gmail.com

You, Me, and the Sunken Treasure

ISBN: 978-3-96324-477-3

Also available as an e-book.

Published by Ylva Publishing, legal entity of Ylva Verlag, e.Kfr.

Ylva Verlag, e.Kfr.
Owner: Astrid Ohletz
Am Kirschgarten 2
65830 Kriftel
Germany

www.ylva-publishing.com

First edition: 2021

Credits
Edited by Gill McKnight and Alissa McGowan
Cover Design and Print Layout by Streetlight Graphics

www.ingramcontent.com/pod-product-compliance
Ingram Content Group UK Ltd.
Pitfield, Milton Keynes, MK11 3LW, UK
UKHW021910190726
13853UKWH00002B/598

9 783963 244773